ALL JUST GLASS

ALL JUST GLASS

Amelia Atwater-Rhodes

ALL JUST GLASS

DELACORTE PRESS

Copyright © 2011 by Amelia Atwater-Rhodes
All rights reserved. Published in the United States by Delacorte Press, an imprint of
Random House Children's Books, a division of Random House, Inc., New York.

Delacorte Press is a registered trademark and the colophon
is a trademark of Random House, Inc.

Visit us on the Web! www.randomhouse.com/teens

Educators and librarians, for a variety of teaching tools, visit us at
www.randomhouse.com/teachers

Library of Congress Cataloging-in-Publication Data
Atwater-Rhodes, Amelia.
All just glass / by Amelia Atwater-Rhodes. — 1st ed.
p. cm.
Companion to Shattered mirror.
Summary: Turned into a vampire by the boy she thought she loved, seventeen-year-old Sarah,
daughter of a powerful line of vampire-hunting witches, is now hunted by her older sister
Adia, who has been given the assignment to kill Sarah.
ISBN 978-0-385-73752-4 (hc) — ISBN 978-0-385-90671-5 (lib. bdg.) —
ISBN 978-0-375-89807-5 (ebook)
[1. Vampires—Fiction. 2. Witches—Fiction. 3. Sisters—Fiction.] I. Title.
PZ7.A8925Al 2011
[Fic]—dc22
2010003772

The text of this book is set in 12-point Loire.

Book design by Jinna Shin

Printed in the United States of America

10 9 8 7 6 5 4 3 2 1

First Edition

All Just Glass *is dedicated to mothers and families trying their best. They say we don't choose our families, but I am one of the few who could never have chosen better than I received. I know how lucky I am.*

Along that line, I need to thank my sister Rachel for helping me revise the first chapter samples of All Just Glass *(as well as* Token of Darkness *and* Poison Tree *). Rachel, you were my very first reader and editor, since I was in sixth grade and gave you* Red Moon. *Your honest support has always encouraged me to tackle new challenges and to be better than I ever would have been without you.*

Thank you as well and as always to my writing group, who took so much abuse as part of the revision process of All Just Glass. *Bri, Sha, Mop, Zim and Mace . . . you put up with so much from me. I never could have brought AJG to this point without you.*

Finally, once more I must thank the Office of Letters and Light for bringing us NaNoWriMo. I spent about ten years trying to write All Just Glass. *I finally put aside everything I had written and, without referring to any notes or prose from the past decade, went for 50k/30 days in November of 2008. I have never been happier with the results of slightly bending the rules.*

I Have a Rendezvous with Death

I have a rendezvous with Death
At some disputed barricade,
When Spring comes back with rustling shade
And apple-blossoms fill the air—
I have a rendezvous with Death
When Spring brings back blue days and fair.

It may be he shall take my hand
And lead me into his dark land
And close my eyes and quench my breath—
It may be I shall pass him still.
I have a rendezvous with Death
On some scarred slope of battered hill,
When Spring comes round again this year
And the first meadow-flowers appear.

God knows 'twere better to be deep
Pillowed in silk and scented down,
Where love throbs out in blissful sleep,
Pulse nigh to pulse, and breath to breath,
Where hushed awakenings are dear . . .
But I've a rendezvous with Death
At midnight in some flaming town,
When Spring trips north again this year,
And I to my pledged word am true,
I shall not fail that rendezvous.

—Alan Seeger

CHAPTER 1

SATURDAY, 5:52 A.M.

THE RINGING IN her ears surely was the sound of the world shattering. It was louder than the November air whistling outside as it tore leaves the color of fire and blood from the trees, and louder than the hum of the Chevy's engine as Adianna Vida pressed the gas pedal down further, accelerating past sixty . . . seventy . . .

Pushing eighty miles per hour, she twisted the dial on her satellite radio, turning the music up in the hope that it would drown out every other sound and thought. She wasn't even sure what she was listening to. It didn't matter.

She wondered if this was why Sarah had always been drawn to fast, flashy cars. Adia went for vehicles that drew no particular attention, cars she could get on short lease terms and trade in frequently, and she had always thought it was a little silly when Sarah picked out something that turned heads whenever she drove up.

But that was the way Sarah was.

Adia glanced at her instrument panel and realized the needle had just passed ninety. Where were the cops who were supposed to be patrolling this highway, anyway? Wasn't there anyone out here still serving and protecting?

She flexed her left hand, clenching her jaw to control a wince as she did so. Two of the fingers were broken. They wouldn't wrap around the steering wheel. The arm was still sore from a minor fracture she had received half a week earlier. She would have double-checked that the hastily tied bandage on her arm was still in place, but she didn't think it was a good idea to take her one good hand off the wheel, even to make sure she wasn't bleeding again.

At least the other guy looked worse . . . though that would have been more comforting if the "other guy" hadn't been a large bay window and some kind of ugly garden statue she had hit on her way down.

But it wasn't a complete loss. She had learned what she had needed to learn.

She had learned the last thing she had *wanted* to learn.

Adianna Vida, now the *only* child of Dominique Vida, matriarch of the ancient line of witches, wished she were still ignorant. It had taken a hell of a fight, but she had finally, unfortunately, throttled the information out of someone.

"Looks like she's decided to live, witch," a bloodbond had told her, the last word like a curse. *"She's staying with Nikolas and*

Kristopher. Not that you'll find them. They've been hunted for more than a century. They know how to take care of themselves."

Sarah was still alive.

No, not Sarah. The creature who existed now *looked* like Adia's little sister, but she wasn't a witch anymore; she was a vampire. She had woken at sundown and had hunted. No one had been able to tell Adia who the victim had been, but Sarah's change had been traumatic, which meant the first hunt would have been fierce. She had probably killed.

And then she had decided to live as a vampire.

To *continue* as a vampire, at least.

Which proved it really wasn't Sarah, right? A daughter of Vida waking to find herself a monster should have ended it at that moment. She should have known that stopping herself *then*, before the vampiric power twisted her too badly, was the only way she could protect the helpless victims she would inevitably end up hurting in the future. But she hadn't.

Before Adia could learn any more, another bloodbond had leapt forward and sent them both through the window. Adia had wanted to fight at that point but had already found the information she needed, and knew that Dominique would disapprove of her lingering.

Realizing she was approaching her exit, she slowed— probably more abruptly than she should have, but who cared? It was six in the morning on a Saturday, and she hadn't seen another car in nearly half an hour. She was almost home, and when she pulled into the driveway, she would have to be fully under control.

She turned the radio down to barely a whisper, until she

could hear the mournful wind again. In front of her mother's house, the trees were already nearly bare, except for a few golden leaves they still managed to cling desperately to. She sympathized; some part of her had been ripped away, as well, when she had let her sister die.

It took her two tries to get the car door open with the damage to her arms. The frigid air that rushed in to replace the warmth in the car was bracing and helped her calm her thoughts. She managed not to limp as she approached the front door.

Her mother was waiting for her in the kitchen, at the antique oak table where Adia had spent countless hours as a child studying ancient Vida laws.

Forty years old, Dominique had been the only child of her father's second wife. She had survived the deaths of her parents, her sister, a niece and a nephew closer to her age than her sister had been, and Sarah and Adia's father, and all Adia had ever seen from her was stoicism and the grim acceptance that a hunter's life was dangerous. Her practical short blond hair had occasional bits of gray and her Vida-blue eyes were perhaps a little more tired, but she still stood as if carrying the weight of the world were simply a task she had to accept.

And at that moment, she wasn't alone.

Adia's cousin, Zachary, had a spread of weaponry in front of him and was in the process of cleaning and polishing the collection of knives as Adia walked in. His blond hair and immaculate appearance were a marked contrast with the slightly scruffy features and dark hair of Michael Arun, who was flipping through the heavy tome of pictures and notes on known vampires.

Michael was from another line, but he was still a witch. The Arun line wasn't known for self-control or following all the rules, and Adia had never quite been able to relax her guard around Michael because of the vampiric taint to his aura, but at least he was a hunter. The Vida and Arun lines had fought side by side for generations, so his presence wasn't surprising, despite the hour. Most vampire hunters were nearly as nocturnal as their prey.

Adia was startled, however, to see Hasana Smoke sitting stiffly across the table from Zachary and staring pale-faced at the weaponry as her daughter Caryn read a paperback romance novel in the corner. Smoke witches, though every bit as respected as Vidas, were healers. They wouldn't engage in a fight even to protect their own lives, and they usually showed up at the Vida household only if someone was hurt.

More unusual still was the presence of Evan Marinitch. Nearing fifty, Evan had a lean body that made him seem younger. He was at that moment perched on the counter, hazel eyes brimming with fatigue and disapproval. The Marinitch line sometimes included hunters, but that wasn't their primary vocation. They were mostly scholars. Though technically kin to the Vida, Arun and Smoke lines, the Marinitch line kept to itself most of the time.

All the surviving lines were represented. Had Dominique called them to witness Sarah's trial, only to have them arrive just to hear about her death?

How had everything happened so fast? Two weeks before, Sarah had been complaining—softly, when Dominique couldn't hear—about having to move from New York City to the small suburb of Acton, Massachusetts. Ten days ago, Adia had discovered that Sarah was being socially polite with two of the vampires who attended her school. The relationship had grown dangerously close before Adia even realized it was happening.

Two days ago, Dominique had bound Sarah's powers in anticipation of a trial for crimes against the line. Alone and without her magic, Sarah had gone up against one of the infamous vampires of the modern age in an attempt to clear her name.

And then . . . Adia looked at the clock on the mantel. Just twenty-four hours ago, Adia had walked away and let that creature change her little sister into a monster. He had claimed that it was the only way to save her life, and in that moment, Adia had let herself believe the lie that her sister could still be saved.

But twelve hours ago, that monster had awoken and fed, and now—

Oh, god.

Adia had memorized pages and pages of Vida law, and now at last the one that mattered came to mind. The other lines weren't here to witness a trial.

"Adia, what have you learned?" Dominique asked.

Hasana looked over her shoulder at Adia and her eyes widened. She shot to her feet. "You're injured—"

Adia shook off the healer's concern and answered Dominique's question.

"According to numerous sources, Sarah has chosen to . . . live." She hesitated before the last word, knowing that it wasn't exactly what she meant. "She has fed, and is now staying with Nikolas and Kristopher, wherever they are."

Hasana sagged with relief. Evan closed his eyes with a

wince, undoubtedly knowing what was coming. Zachary nodded, his expression remote, and Michael paled. Michael Arun had always been a mystery to Adia, but he and Sarah had been close. They had even dated for a while, before deciding they were good partners when hunting but weren't compatible romantically.

Dominique didn't even blink. Impeccably controlled as always, she simply said, "Well."

She stood, and her gaze swept the assembled witches.

"My daughter is dead," she announced. "I know her killers."

She placed on the table a pencil drawing of the twin vampires Nikolas and Kristopher, provided by the fiends themselves. The one called Kristopher had courted Sarah with drawings. He had befriended her, and Sarah had let him, despite Adia's begging her to be careful. She had always been headstrong.

"As a child of Macht, I am invoking the Rights of Kin," Dominique said. Adia had known that it was coming, but she still consciously had to keep her expression controlled so she wouldn't flinch. "Please witness."

Now Hasana paled visibly. Apparently, she had finally caught up to the rest of them. A Smoke witch's training was not as intensive as a Vida's. They were taught to heal and tended to be less aware of the laws that governed all their lines, but Hasana's reaction made it clear that she recognized the name.

"Dominique, don't do this," Hasana said. "Or at least give yourself some time to reconsider. Sarah isn't—"

"Sarah *is* dead," Dominique said flatly. "There is a vampire out there wearing her shape, her skin, but that creature is no witch, no Vida."

Zachary spoke first, as the eldest of the Vida line after Dominique. He said simply, "Witnessed."

"Is this truly necessary?" Evan asked.

"Yes," Zachary replied.

Evan Marinitch drew a breath and said, "Witnessed." He swallowed thickly. "We have only one hunter in our line this generation. My son. I will see that he joins you."

"Dominique, *please,*" Hasana begged. All eyes turned toward her, the witches waiting. "Think about—"

"No," Dominique interrupted, her blue gaze cold as ice. "My line has been savaged this generation." She swept the room with her eyes, catching each gaze in turn. "Rose was bled dry as part of a sick game after she walked into a trap, after her husband was stabbed with his own knife by a bloodbond who *claimed* she was allied with SingleEarth, and their daughter Jacqueline was slaughtered despite having tried to give up our ways. Her son Richard, who was only a *child*, was taken—and god only knows what happened to him—and never seen again." Zachary was one of the few who held Dominique's gaze as she referred to the events that had brought him, an orphan, into their household when Adia had been a baby. "And then the father of my children was tortured to death and dropped on our front steps."

Hasana looked away. Caryn seemed about to argue, but her mother put a hand on her shoulder; the young witch shook off the touch and stormed out of the room.

Still, Dominique was not done.

"Through the generations we have played it safe, and not sought personal vengeance—and now we who stand in this room are the last of the Vida line. The least we can do for our fallen kin is destroy the creature inhabiting Sarah's skin before it can use her shell to commit crimes no Vida could ever condone. So I call on the ancient laws now to help me, so I can bury my daughter and let her rest in peace."

No one said another word; there was no point in arguing. This was a formality, not a choice to be debated.

At last, Hasana choked out the word: "Witnessed."

They turned to Michael next. Like the Vidas, the Arun line had faced hardships recently. They had never been prolific, and in the past century many had been born completely human, with no power to speak of. Michael was the last witch of his line. When he spoke, his voice was barely a whisper.

"Witnessed."

The Rights of Kin were one of the oldest of the Macht witches' laws, spoken by the very first Vida after her mother was brutally slain before her eyes, and passed down orally for centuries before written language was developed. They applied to every living line descended from that ancient tribe but had not been called upon in more than a thousand years.

When witch-kin is slain, there shall be no safe haven, no higher law to protect the guilty. Every hunter shall turn her blade to the task, and there shall be no rest until those responsible have been slain. These are the Rights of Kin.

"Adianna." She wasn't being asked to witness; Zachary had already spoken for their line. A tremor of nervousness passed through her as Dominique gave her orders. "I am putting you in charge of this hunt. Nikolas and Kristopher are necessary targets, but your highest goal is the creature wearing Sarah's form. I want you to find her, and put a knife in her heart. Is that clear?"

Adia glanced toward Zachary, but he had dropped his gaze back to the blades before him, accepting Dominique's delegation of power without question.

Zachary was older, twenty-six years to Adia's nineteen, but he had been a child when his mother and his two siblings had been lost. Dominique had become matriarch of their line, and Adia would inherit that title from her, so it was natural that she would want to put Adia in charge of this mission.

What Dominique could never know was that Adia had already failed once, when she had turned around and let one of *them* give Sarah his blood. Adia had been there. She could have ended this travesty before it began. But she hadn't been strong enough.

Now the command had been given and there was only one possible response.

"Yes, and I will obey," she replied, her words formal despite her silent dread. She had to make herself strong enough. Anything else would be a betrayal of her line.

Michael turned his face away as if he couldn't stand to look at her anymore. Evan stood and said flatly, "I will send my son to you," before walking out the door.

Dominique stepped back and glanced at the clock before saying to her daughter, "If there is a next generation, you will be its matriarch, but I've held you in my shadow longer than

I should have. The hunters you will be working with are your peers, so it is right that you lead them now. I will get out of the way unless you call me in." Then, in as close to an admission of weakness as Adia had ever heard her mother utter, she added, "For now, I need to rest."

Adia did not think Dominique had truly *slept* since she had bound Sarah's powers two days before. She had given good reasons for Adia's leading this hunt, but Adia suspected there was one more: Dominique was tired, in body and heart.

Adia nodded, though it felt odd to have her mother looking to her for permission. "You rest. We need you strong. Once you're up, you can start calling your contacts." Dominique's network of hunters and informants was impressive. Adia knew only some of them.

Only once Dominique left did Hasana approach Adia to say, "I should set those fingers before they start to heal that way. It looks like you need stitches in your arm, too."

"Where's Caryn?" Adia asked, wondering why Hasana hadn't gone to check on her daughter.

"She brought her own car," Hasana said, moving to examine the wounds while she spoke. "She thought we were being called for Sarah's trial, and insisted on coming to speak on her behalf."

Caryn herself had nearly been brought to trial not long before for far more severe crimes than Sarah had ever committed; if she had been a hunter, and not a healer, she never could have justified her actions. But maybe she had thought she could justify Sarah's.

Adia sat while Hasana set and splinted her broken fingers,

then put six stitches in her upper arm. The healer's power numbed the pain from the injury and the needle going into and out of damaged flesh, leaving Adia with a disconnected sensation. In some ways she would rather have the pain than this sense that the skin the healer was stitching wasn't really hers, but instead belonged to a stranger.

After a few minutes, Michael came to the table. Zachary looked up. The three hunters exchanged wary glances.

"Where do we begin?" Zachary asked.

Adia shook her head, just barely. She had some ideas, but they couldn't be spoken in front of Hasana. Once the healer was gone, the hunters would begin to make their plans.

CHAPTER 2

SATURDAY, 5:54 A.M.

SARAH SAT ON her feet so she could look across the scarred old oak table at her sister. The year between them might as well have been a century, if one judged by the awe with which Sarah regarded Adia— or the childlike haughtiness the eight-year-old demonstrated in response.

"It's 'make no deals, barter no honor,'" Adia corrected her gently.

Sarah ran the words through her head, whispering them under her breath before repeating them out loud, and then asking, "What does 'barter' mean?"

Adia glanced up through the doorway, to where their mother was demonstrating a new fighting form to Zachary, before she answered, "Like if I agree to do the dishes if you'll do my homework."

"Then . . . I should stop doing that."

"It's only with them. Not us," Adia explained. "We can be trusted, so it's okay."

Sarah frowned, trying to make sense of the passage Dominique had assigned her to memorize. Why did it all have to be written with big words and fancy sentences?

Her gaze drifted from the book to a streak of color on the table. The kitchen window had a panel of decorative cut glass, and at that moment, the rising sun was hitting it just right to make tiny rainbows all around the room. The spring day was windy, and the new leaves on the trees outside rustled, making the light move and the rainbows dance on the table.

"Sarah, Adia," Dominique admonished them, appearing like magic in Sarah's instant of inattention.

"Sorry, Mother," Adia said while Sarah tried to decide if she really had seen movement through the window.

It had probably been a squirrel or a stray cat, but she said, "I think I saw someone outside."

Seizing the excuse to get out of her chair before her mother could forbid her, she sprang to her feet and bounced across the room, stretching her seven-year-old body. She had pins and needles in her left foot, and that caused her to stumble as she flung open the door.

She saw the object on the front step, but she couldn't stop her forward momentum before she tripped over it. She fell. Her eyes focused, and understanding came in flashes. Red blood, sticky. Clammy texture under her hands—dead skin. Glazed eyes staring toward her, seeing nothing. There was blood . . . everywhere . . . from what seemed like millions of cuts on his arms and throat and chest.

And it was her father.

And he was dead.

The scream bubbled up through a throat tight with horror and came out strangled.

"Sarah Vida!"

Her mother's voice sounded very far away.

Adia grabbed her and dragged her from the doorway. Mother and Zachary worked together to get the body off the front porch before anyone else could see it.

Rainbows danced on his chalk gray and blood-slicked skin.

Sarah Vida woke with a silent shudder. When she had been seven, she had screamed until her throat was raw. Now she did not utter a sound.

She had known that vampires did not create dreams but instead relived their memories when they slept. Knowing was not the same as experiencing, however. Humans and witches alike were capable of having nightmares about the bad times. She had dreamed about her father's death before. She had thought that was what people meant when they said vampires dreamed the past.

But dreams weren't like *this*, with every detail as vivid as it had been then.

Why couldn't she have dreamed about going to the butterfly garden with her father? Or about the way he had smiled whenever she had correctly reproduced a complicated fighting form? Her best memories of him involved hot cocoa on cold nights when her mother was away hunting, and his singing her to sleep—again, on nights when her mother was not there to stop him. He hadn't been a Vida; he hadn't needed to follow their obsessive code of perfection and self-control. He hadn't even been a witch—just a damn fine hunter, one who had earned even Dominique's respect.

Any memory of him alive would have been welcome. Why did she have to dream his *death*?

It didn't matter that her mother had tracked down and killed his murderers. There was no way to avenge the slaughter of a child's innocence. With her father's death, her childhood had ended.

She drew a deep breath, dropping into old habits meant to focus the body and mind, but she had no pulse to regulate and the air that came into her lungs was useless to her.

She rubbed her hands over her arms, trying to remind herself of her physical body and remove herself from memories, and her palms passed over pale skin and paler scars. The lines were faint now: a strand of ivy etched into her wrist, a rose on one shoulder and the name Nikolas on the other. There had been other wounds, including another name—Kristopher—but they had been too new and had healed completely when she had been—

She leaned back against the wall as it all returned.

The previous day, she had come to the home of one of the most infamous vampires in history, planning to kill him or die trying. What she hadn't expected was that she would die, and then wake up as the sun set, with no pulse, and blood on her lips.

She shuddered. Not long before, if anyone had asked her what she would do if she were changed, she would have said without hesitation, *I'll do the right thing. A daughter of Vida would never allow herself to become a monster.*

Now she didn't know.

All she knew was that Nikolas and Kristopher—the two vampires who had killed her, albeit somewhat accidentally—had brought her here to their home to wait for her meeting at SingleEarth.

SingleEarth, an international organization founded by the Smoke line of witches in the early nineteen hundreds, was dedicated to the concept that all the sentient creatures of this world were capable of peaceful coexistence. To that end, they helped immortal and ageless creatures function in a mortal world. They did everything, from providing passports and setting up bank accounts to creating updated birth and death certificates as necessary. Sarah needed them to help her find a place to stay.

Kristopher had offered to let her live with them for as long as she liked, of course, but she wanted to find her own path first. She didn't want to give up on independence and move in, even with the vampire who had taught her that not all of his kind was as evil as she had been raised to believe.

His kind; her kind now.

My kind. The words echoed in her mind, and again she tried to draw a breath to steady herself. It brought the smell of browning butter to her. Someone, probably her housemate, Christine, was cooking downstairs.

Christine was a fine example of why the hunters generally thought vampires like Nikolas deserved to die. Like Sarah, Christine wore Nikolas's marks on her arms. Hunters saw them as a kind of brand, left by a sadist whose arrogance led him to sign his kills. Vampires saw them as a claim, one they could not say they didn't notice, that marked the human as under Nikolas's protection.

Normally no one would dare harm anyone who wore those marks, but Christine had been caught in the power struggle between Nikolas and another of his kind, an ancient vampire named Kaleo. By the time Nikolas had been alerted to Christine's situation, Kaleo had nearly driven her mad.

The sun was only hinting at rising, but nevertheless, Sarah found Christine in the kitchen, beating eggs while mushrooms and peppers crackled in butter on the stove. Dressed in gray sweatpants and a black pajama top, Christine was humming some upbeat pop song as she worked, her eyes half closed as one of her bare feet tapped on the floor.

And she smelled good, Sarah realized. It wasn't browning butter and sautéing mushrooms and peppers that had snared Sarah's attention; it was the rich, metallic smell beyond all that, beneath the flesh. . . .

Sarah shoved herself backward before Christine even noticed her. In the living room, out of sight of the mostly human girl, she leaned against the wall.

She shoved the craving back down. Her body, which had momentarily gloried in the prospect of sustenance, screamed at her that she needed to *hunt*, to *feed*, but she ignored that, too, until the pain that scraped across her flesh and along the inside of her veins was nothing to her.

How *could* she? Christine had been victimized and brutalized, but for just a moment, Sarah had seen her, smelled her and thought of her as *food*.

She would have to be more careful. She had a sense of how long a vampire could safely go without blood. Most of them lacked the self-control to refrain from hunting more frequently—

killing, even—but she had been a daughter of Vida. Pain was nothing. Soon the vampires at SingleEarth would be able to teach her how they survived without killing; they would teach her how to feed safely, maybe on animals, the way Kristopher had for fifty years before she met him. Until then, she wouldn't let the bloodlust control her even a moment more.

Now fully under control, she stepped back into the kitchen. Her face reflected none of the horror of her dream or the agony of the bloodlust as she said, "Good morning, Christine."

Christine turned with a grin and a glance out the window. "I guess it is. I'm making an omelet. Would you like some?"

Sarah smiled and shook her head. "I don't think it would do much for me."

Christine shrugged. "You might not need it to fill your stomach, but Nikolas tells me that a lot of vampires enjoy the taste or smell of food, even if it doesn't provide sustenance. He says it's one of the things that make eternity worthwhile." Maybe in another century Sarah would agree, but for the moment it seemed like a terrible waste of food. She didn't have to answer, though, since Christine glanced at the clock and said, "You keep odd hours for a vampire."

"It might take me some time to get it right," Sarah said.

Like most vampires, she had slept all day following her change. She had woken disoriented, nearly mindless. Kristopher had bared his own throat, knowing that she needed blood to survive but risked killing any human she fed on in that state. It had been enough to help complete the change, but she had still been exhausted. She lay down, expecting to close her eyes for just a minute, and now it was nearly dawn.

She had to get to SingleEarth before it got later. Even as a newly changed vampire, she knew that her energy levels would only plummet more as the sun rose higher.

"Are you all right here for a bit?" Sarah asked.

Christine hesitated but then nodded.

"I'll be back soon."

Sarah dressed in a knee-length black skirt and a white blouse—clothes borrowed from Christine. Nikolas decorated himself and his house in combinations of black and white, and Christine had taken to styling herself in the same. Sarah swore that when she bought herself new clothes, they would be decorated with rainbows.

She stared at herself in the full-length mirror as she brushed her blond hair and braided it back, out of her way. At least she had found a long-sleeved shirt that hid the scars on her arms, but the vampiric black eyes where she was used to seeing Vida-blue ones chilled her. She barely resisted an urge to slam a palm into the mirror's surface and shatter it to send the image away.

She remembered doing something similar when she was seven. Hysterical, still screaming after the discovery of her father, she had thrown anything that had come to hand. When she had run out of things to throw, she had turned toward the window. The bright rainbows around the room, dancing over her father's dead flesh, had offended her. She had slammed a fist with all her strength through the decorative cut-glass panels.

She had torn her hand to ribbons and broken three fingers. Her mother had allowed the hand to be set and bandaged but had bound Sarah's power so she would heal at a nearly human rate, to teach her the consequences of emotional reactions. Of losing control.

She was supposed to have learned her lesson. Now all those years of struggling for flawless discipline, training to be *perfect*, had left her in a refuge provided to her by the vampire who had been her enemy so recently she wore his marks in her flesh— and would for the rest of eternity.

CHAPTER 3

SATURDAY, 6:12 A.M.

ADIA FELT A little giddy as she and Zachary crossed the threshold of the local SingleEarth Haven.

The compound was less than fifteen minutes away from their house, but Adia had never been there. Dominique had chosen to live close to SingleEarth's healers, but they normally came to the house so hunters did not need to profane Single-Earth's cherished lands.

It wasn't that hunters weren't *allowed* at SingleEarth, exactly, but they certainly were not welcome.

As the name implied, this was supposed to be a safe place. Those inside were protected from persecution, whether by hunters or others of their own kind. The Vida, Arun and Marinitch lines had sworn to honor that agreement, even though

SingleEarth's dominion caused a great deal of frustration. There was nothing quite so frustrating as knowing that someone in this place had information, or a history of slaughter, and not being able to do anything about it.

Everything had changed when Dominique had invoked the Rights, though.

Adia pitied Michael a little. It had seemed like a bad idea to bring someone as volatile as an Arun to SingleEarth, so Michael was assigned to check the house where Kristopher and his sister, Nissa, had previously stayed.

It wasn't *entirely* busywork. The witches were bound to tell the others of their lines about the Rights of Kin, but no one would have told Nissa. If she had any brains at all, she would have disappeared when she'd learned that her brothers had tangled with a Vida, but maybe she wasn't that bright. Maybe Michael would get lucky.

Adia doubted it. Their prey was much more likely to have gone somewhere like SingleEarth, where they would assume that the witches' own laws would protect them. Therefore, Adia much preferred to be here, with Zachary. Zachary had moved out when he was sixteen and Adia was nine, so they had never been as close as siblings. But when they exchanged a glance at that moment, Adia could see that he was as thrilled by their new freedom as she was. She knew that her expression did not show her excitement—she had trained too long and hard to let such an emotion betray her—but her cousin would see it in her eyes just as she could see it in his.

Sarah would have.

And just like that, the excitement came crashing down.

"You take the resident halls," she said softly. "I'll check the common rooms."

Vampires had the irritating ability to disappear and travel any distance in the blink of an eye. A well-trained witch of their line could disrupt that power, but to do so required touch, which meant it was normally hard to catch someone who wasn't arrogant enough to come out and fight. They would have only one chance at this, before their target learned that the Rights of Kin were in play, so it would be best to cover as much ground as quickly as possible. This early in the morning, most of SingleEarth's vampires were still awake and social. Adia would have been happy to wait until they were curled up asleep in bed, which most would be within the next couple of hours, but she did not want to risk waiting and having word reach their targets.

After they split up, Adia was the one who got lucky. She found Nissa in one of the art rooms, receiving instruction on stone carving from a girl who reeked of a vampiric taint. She was not a vampire, but a bloodbond to someone old, and powerful.

"Nissa?"

The vampire lifted black eyes as Adia said her name. A sad smile crossed her face, but she walked fearlessly toward Adia.

"Adianna, right?" she asked. "You're Sarah's sister."

Adia nodded tightly. Unfortunately, Nissa wasn't dumb. Adia doubted she would say anything helpful without coercion.

"And you're . . . Kristopher's sister," Adia said. At least for a little while recently, Kristopher had pretended to be human. To be something other than evil. His little game had started this whole disaster.

"Are younger sisters as much trouble as brothers?" Nissa

asked, shaking her head. "If you were hoping to get in touch with Sarah, I can pass a message on for you."

Adia winced. She couldn't help it.

Nissa stepped forward and put a comforting hand on Adia's shoulder. Adia resisted the instinct to pull back, instead letting her power seep subtly over Nissa's, tangling it enough to hold her in place when she decided the wise course of action was to flee.

"I know what you're going through," Nissa said. "I'm sure your whole world has been turned upside down. But it gets better. I don't approve of a lot of the choices Nikolas and Kristopher make, but they're still my brothers, you know?"

Adia couldn't handle too much more of this. "Do you know where I would find Sarah?"

"She and Christine are—" Nissa stopped and frowned, her body going tense. Her eyes searched Adia's face. "Are you looking for her because she's your sister, or because she's your prey?"

Adia let herself look offended and innocent, eyes wide. "I just want to see her," she said. It didn't hurt to try, right?

Nissa looked ambivalent. "I can pass on a message, and see if she would be willing to meet you here," she suggested.

Adia considered it. If Sarah didn't know that the Rights were in play, she might show up, believing herself safe. On the other hand, she was smart and knew Vida law as well as Adia did. If she received such an invitation, she would wonder why Adia was extending it, and might deduce what was going on, at which point Adia would have lost her best lead.

Adia didn't need Nissa to tell her anything, really. The twins protected their kin.

"I need you to come with me," Adia said.

Nissa looked shocked. "You're hunting her," she said. "You're really . . . You would really kill your own *sister*?"

Adia was sure she could take Nissa down in a fight, but with Zachary's help, she could take Nissa alive. The twins would undoubtedly come to avenge her, but the hunters had more leverage if she was alive. Adia sent out a thread of power to Zachary, prompting him to come back to her, and answered Nissa's question as a stall tactic.

"In a heartbeat," she said, "before I let her kill anyone else."

She was glad her voice was steady. She *did* believe her words but was still pleased that her voice didn't betray that her heart-beat was rapid with fear of the moment when she would have to follow through with the promise.

"Not all of us are killers," Nissa snapped. She wasn't running yet only because she didn't know she needed to. She probably thought she could convince Adia to change her mind.

"Oh?" Adia answered, letting her anger into her voice. People became more involved in emotional arguments than calm ones; she wanted Nissa's guard down. "And what about your brothers—you know, the ones Sarah is staying with? The ones teaching her how to *hunt*." Anger was a double-edged sword, of course. The emotion was real as she spat the last word. As she continued, she sensed that Zachary was circling to slip in behind Nissa from the opposite door. "In fact, what about *you*? You're here at SingleEarth. I can feel how weak you are. Tell me you've never in your century and a half taken a human life."

Nissa hesitated, as Adia had known she would. Adia

couldn't sense death on her, but it wasn't possible for a vampire to live so long and never kill.

"Really," Adia added, "please do. I would love to believe it."

Were those words honest? She didn't know.

Nissa yelped as Zachary reached her and grabbed her wrists. He was better with raw energy than Adia was, so she relinquished her hold over the vampire's power.

"How can you live with yourself?" Adia asked her, wondering if there was any grain of similarity between them. Nissa was the one who had changed Nikolas into a vampire. Adia did not know the circumstances of that decision, and she didn't care. Maybe Nissa hadn't known what Nikolas would turn into then, but how could she do nothing *now*?

Defiantly, Nissa snapped, "I have my brothers."

Nissa tried to wrench her wrists out of Zachary's grip, and he shifted, putting one hand over the power center in her throat.

"I can kill you this way," Zachary said flatly. "Adia and I agreed that out of respect for SingleEarth, we would rather let you live, but that is assuming you do not give us trouble. We need you to come with us now."

Nissa became very still. "You're not allowed. Not here."

"That was then," Zachary answered. "This is now. We—"

A bloodbond blindsided both of them, attacking while Adia's attention was focused on Nissa. The girl probably weighed ninety pounds, but she fought in a suicidal whirlwind of shouting and fury that made it obvious her stature was not an indication of her strength.

She made a deep slash on Zachary's arm with an X-Acto

knife. He had to let go of Nissa to defend himself. Adia made a grab at the vampire when Zachary dropped her, but she was too slow.

The bloodbond shouted, "Go!"

Nissa disappeared.

"I recognize you," Zachary said as the bloodbond fell into a defensive crouch, the knife in one hand. The mad assault had obviously been meant to distract them from Nissa, and it had worked. Now she was waiting for them to make the next move. "Heather. You're Kaleo's pet."

Adia hadn't recognized the face, but she knew the name. She wasn't sure how old Kaleo's favorite bloodbond was, but clearly she was trained well enough to leap in front of hunters' blades to protect one of Kaleo's fledglings. Of course, blood-bonds tended to be fanatically loyal like that.

"Better a pet than a mindless tool," Heather spat. "How *dare* you threaten Nissa?"

At a glance from Zachary, Adia moved forward. The action was a feint, but it was enough to draw Heather's attention. The instant the bloodbond struck out with the knife, Zachary swept in behind her. He caught her wrist in one hand, control-ling the knife, and wrapped his other hand around the front of her throat as he had with Nissa. The following ripple of power slapped Adia like a burst of frigid air, and then Heather went limp and the knife clattered to the floor.

Kicking the weapon away, Zachary heaved the bloodbond into a fireman's carry. Adia looked around and hastily found some duct tape and cotton balls, which she used to create a makeshift bandage for the gash across Zachary's arm. He let her do so without putting Heather down.

The slight delay gave Hasana Smoke time to emerge. Adia wondered what had taken her so long.

"You're not taking that girl out of here," Hasana protested.

"I don't see why not," Zachary replied. He swayed a little and shifted to lean on the doorway as if bored, disguising his weakness as apathy. Adia was pretty sure she was the only one who would be able to tell the difference.

"Much as I hate it, I know the Rights give you the authority to storm in here and threaten harmless people like Nissa," Hasana said. "But they don't give you permission to kidnap anyone you feel like."

"First," Adia said, "the Rights of Kin give us the authority to follow any path to our targets we must. This one jumped into the fray to protect Nissa. Ergo, she has a connection to that group. Second, she attacked us. She violated SingleEarth's commandments and is therefore not protected by its haven. Zachary, let's go."

She led the way. Zachary followed. She wondered how much power he had just burned, and what it had cost him. Knocking a human unconscious without killing or doing permanent damage required a kind of precision that Adia found difficult. Sarah had always been pretty good at that kind of thing, but doing it instantly to a bloodbond with Heather's level of strength required an incredible amount of power.

Sure enough, the moment they returned to Zachary's car, he dumped Heather into the backseat, handed Adia the keys and collapsed into the passenger seat.

"Are you all right?" Adia asked.

He nodded. "I'll be fine." He closed his eyes and rubbed at his temples. "It would be more comfortable if you took a crowbar to my head, but the headache will pass, eventually."

"What will we do with Heather?" Adia asked, checking around the car as she started it, in case any more crazed Single-Earth members were planning to attack them. For now, it seemed like the rest were giving them a wide berth.

Zachary shrugged. "We can get information from her. And even if we can't, Kaleo will probably come for her; he's had her too long to abandon her without it looking like weakness. Even if he's not *directly* part of our current target, I wouldn't mind having a shot at that sadist."

Adia was occasionally worried that Zachary, so far as she could tell, wouldn't mind "having a shot at" a bunny if it were sufficiently connected to vampires. She didn't speak the thought out loud, though; about Kaleo, they were in agreement.

Zachary was the perfect Vida: a cool, controlled hunter who never let himself be distracted in a fight and never let emotion get in the way. Dominique should have put him in charge of hunting down Sarah—Sarah's killers. But Adia suspected that Dominique hadn't chosen her for her skills, but to clearly determine her loyalty. No one would ever doubt Zachary that way.

Adia resisted the urge to floor the accelerator as she merged onto the highway. Zachary couldn't know she was torn inside. He couldn't know that Adianna Vida, oldest and now only daughter of Dominique Vida, wasn't what she appeared.

He couldn't know she was scared—no, terrified.

You would really kill your own sister?

Nissa's accusation echoed through her thoughts.

Failure in this hunt would likely mean the end of their line. The notion of putting a blade between Sarah's ribs made Adia's stomach twist, but Dominique was right that they couldn't continue this way. The Vida line had survived since the dawn of the human species, despite eras of famine, Inquisition and war. If their generation was going to be the last, so be it. She wouldn't shame thirty thousand years of ancestors by putting down her blade and hiding her head in the sand.

CHAPTER 4

SATURDAY, 6:13 A.M.

CARYN SMOKE, THE youngest daughter of the Smoke line, walked into the meeting room where Sarah waited. Her face was perfectly composed despite the rapid pounding of her heart, which echoed in Sarah's ears. Sarah had never realized that the young healer had such self-control.

"You have to leave," Caryn said. "I'm sorry, but you do. Now. SingleEarth can't give you anything. You have to get out of here, before they come back and look for you."

"What?" Sarah had never liked SingleEarth, but they had welcomed some of the vilest creatures in history, provided they had agreed to reform. How could they turn her away?

Caryn shoved a duffel bag at Sarah. "Here's what I could swipe while they were arguing. I know it isn't much, but it's all I could do." Caryn was pale, and now she balled one hand in her black hair. "I'm sorry I can't help more, but my mother says if I cross them, it could endanger everyone at SingleEarth. You and I weren't close, but I know you can take care of yourself. You've got strong friends now. You'll be okay, if you just *go*."

Sarah disappeared without even the sense to demand an explanation. She wasn't sure where she was going; instant transportation was a vampiric trick she used by instinct instead of intent, and the extra effort of bringing the bag with her made her head spin. She nearly fell as she reappeared, before she was caught and pulled into an embrace.

"Sarah, thank god."

She could feel the wash of emotion that accompanied the words, and knew as she leaned on him that this was Kristopher. When she had first woken as a vampire, he had given her his blood so she would not need to hunt and kill an innocent human. Doing so had opened his mind to her.

She closed her eyes and let him hold her for a moment, while simultaneously trying to shield her mind from his thoughts.

Kristopher had flirted with her before he had known she was a witch; she had allowed it because she could sense in his aura that it had been a long time since he had killed, and because she had assumed he was allied with SingleEarth . . . and because it had been nice to have a friend. She didn't know what might have happened between them if she hadn't been a Vida, and if his brother hadn't reacted violently to what he saw as a threat to Kristopher. As it was, they had never even managed a successful first date before their romance had gone the way of Romeo and Juliet's—except that Romeo and Juliet didn't wake up the next day, leave the crypt and say, "Now what?"

Sarah had chosen to go to SingleEarth because she needed *distance,* so she could learn how to live this new life before she had to figure out what she wanted to do about the relationship she had never intended to die for. Now she could barely hear her own thoughts through his anxiety.

"Nissa told us there were hunters at SingleEarth." That piece of information came from another voice, similar to the first but indefinably different. "We were concerned."

Sarah pulled back, fighting the gentle insistence of Kristopher's arms that encouraged her to stay close, when she heard Nikolas's voice. Looking up, she saw that Christine had also joined them.

She had to get herself under control, not just because she still instinctively wanted to be strong in front of Nikolas, her recent enemy, but because Christine had gone through enough lately. She didn't need to see Sarah panicked.

And maybe she could admit, if just to herself, that having someone else to be strong for helped. As a Vida, she had always existed for others. She had lived and died to fulfill vows written by ancestors thousands of years earlier. She had never hesitated to risk her life to protect the innocent. Her friendship with Nissa and Kristopher had been the first thing she had ever sought for herself.

Look where that had brought her.

"Hunters at SingleEarth?" she echoed. "They're powerless

there." Might Adia have been looking for her? One reason Sarah had gone to SingleEarth was that it was owned by the Smoke witches, and they had treaties so even the Vida line was not obligated to hunt vampires within its walls. She hadn't expected her family to want to see her, but she had wanted to give them an option that would free them from being bound by law to kill her.

Kristopher shook his head, his gaze now as dark as his brother's. "They tried to take Nissa. They threatened to kill her if she didn't cooperate."

Sarah shook her head, horrified and amazed. What was going *on*?

All four of them tensed when another figure appeared in the room. Christine recoiled, her face going pale, and as Sarah moved to comfort her, Nikolas and Kristopher stepped protectively between the newcomer and Sarah and Christine. Did they think she needed to be protected, defended, coddled, as if she were helpless? Or was the position accidental, a result of her moving closer to Christine?

That didn't matter right then. What mattered was that Kaleo Sonyar, the vampire who had just appeared among them, looked *pissed*. The oldest living direct fledgling of Kendra, Kaleo was an apt representation of his line: beautiful, an artist, absolutely mad and capable of undeniable cruelty. He had features like a Roman sculpture—quite literally, since rumors claimed he had modeled for some of those works—and golden blond hair that gave him an angelic cast. The looks were misleading, however. By killing Nissa's father and threatening Nikolas, Kaleo had convinced Nissa to let him change her.

More recently, he had bloodbonded Christine and tortured her for months, mainly to spite Nikolas.

Seeing the anger stark on his aristocratic features now gave Sarah the chills.

"What is going on?" Kaleo demanded.

"I think that's our question for you," Kristopher said. "What are you doing in our home?"

Kaleo spun to face Sarah, which made both boys take a protective step forward. "Your 'family' was in SingleEarth."

"I know. They—"

He shook his head, silencing her explanation. "They took Heather. I demand you three get her back."

"You *demand*?" Nikolas repeated incredulously. "Why would we possibly help you rescue one of *your* bonds? What exactly were you doing while she was fighting hunters, anyway?"

Though Sarah was also surprised that he would *expect* their help, she didn't share Nikolas's shock at the request. She knew what the hunters might do to Heather if Heather refused to give them information.

"She is surrounded by witches waiting for some fool to step in to pick her up," Kaleo said. "I'm not about to be the only fool there. As for why you should help, if Heather hadn't distracted the hunters, they would have taken Nissa instead. And finally, I was in the same place you were: *not* in SingleEarth, where I am very much not welcome, and *not* policing my people in a place where they are supposed to be safe from exactly this kind of assault. Since when has that rule changed?"

Both brothers answered the question by looking to Sarah for explanation. "Sarah?" Kristopher asked.

"SingleEarth's autonomy is a high law among all witch-kin—"

"Which is why I was a little surprised they seem to be *ignoring* it," Kaleo interjected.

Sarah stepped back. It didn't make any *sense* . . . but Caryn had acted like it did. *My mother says if I cross them, it could endanger everyone at SingleEarth.* "Oh, goddess," Sarah whispered as the answer struck her like lightning. Her stomach plummeted. Her chest constricted.

"Sarah?"

She wasn't sure who had spoken. She felt blind. But she remembered the ancient words she had spent many hours studying as a child. A Vida was only given a true blade, crafted by the witches of old and imbued with generations of power, after she had recited and then sworn to all the laws of their line. She could have said the words in her sleep, but the only law applicable in that moment was so ancient she would never have thought anyone would invoke it.

When witch-kin is slain, there shall be no safe haven, no higher law to protect the guilty. Every hunter shall turn her blade to the task, and there shall be no rest until those responsible have been slain.

The Rights of Kin hadn't been called upon since the death of Smoke Madder, thousands of years earlier. The conflict had led to the schism that split the witches into separate lines for the first time, with some obeying the Rights and some swearing a vow of nonviolence and giving up the title of hunter for themselves and all their descendants.

Hunters' deaths were avenged when they could be, but most of the time it was simply accepted that hunters eventually lost their lives, usually to their prey. No one had called on the Rights when the Light line had been extinguished three centuries before, and the Vida line had nearly been forced to the same fate. No one had called on the Rights when Nikolas and Kristopher had killed Elisabeth Vida in the 1850s, or when Zachary's sister Jacqueline had been slaughtered, or when Sarah's father had been bled and dumped on their front step.

Sarah was sitting. When had she sat down?

Kristopher was by her side. Nikolas was still standing close to Kaleo, defensive, and Christine was hovering in the doorway at the opposite side of the room. Her face was tight with fear, but she stood solid, eyes only occasionally flickering back to Kaleo from Sarah.

Sarah recognized the posture. It was loyalty that held her when terror made her want to run. It had to be hard for her to stay in the same room with Kaleo, but she did it anyway.

Sarah wanted to say to her, *Just run. Loyalty isn't worth so much sometimes.*

"The Rights of Kin are ancient, *ancient* Vida law," Sarah said. "Older than the other lines' existences. Older than any living vampires, or recorded civilization, for that matter. They were passed down verbally for centuries, because humanity hadn't yet invented written language."

"Get to the *point*," Kaleo growled.

"Back off!" Kristopher shouted. "Can't you see she's in shock?"

Sarah shook herself. She wasn't in shock; a daughter of Vida didn't have that luxury. She pushed herself to her feet.

"The Rights of Kin can be called upon by any descendant of

Macht—any Vida, Smoke, Arun or Marinitch witch—when their kin is slain. The law requires any other child of Macht to set aside all allegiances and obligations to assist with hunting down the killer. The healers don't have to fight, but they can't offer sanctuary or assistance, either. What Caryn did," she said, thinking out loud as her gaze went to the bag the witch had hastily passed her, "would be enough to get her disowned if anyone learned about it."

"Focus, Vida," Kaleo snapped. "What does this mean, right now, to us?"

Kristopher looked ready to murder him, but the sharp words brought Sarah back to herself. They reminded her of the many times she had reported to Dominique, ignoring fatigue or agony after a particularly grueling fight. She had to be practical and keep her mind on what needed to be done. She couldn't dwell on the lump in her stomach when she wondered why now, of all times, Dominique had called upon this ancient law.

"It means that all witches who hunt will turn their full attention on the ones Dominique considers responsible for my murder. They will call on their allies. They will track down anyone they have ever known to have a connection to the killers, without worrying about messy treaties with SingleEarth or other normally respected neutral havens."

"I don't suppose they care that you are not, in fact, dead," Nikolas said.

Sarah shook her head. "In their eyes, I am."

"And we're your killers," Kristopher added. "That means we need to warn our people. Everyone who wears our marks, or is normally allied with us."

"Is Nissa safe?" Kaleo asked.

"She already had her run-in with the hunters—"

"Yes, I'm aware of that," the Roman interrupted. "I assume she came to you after. Is she safe?"

"Yes," Nikolas replied. "We're not stupid. We didn't know about the Rights, but the hunters threatened to kill her. It wasn't subtle. She's gone to ground."

Kaleo nodded and then looked back at Sarah. "What will these hunters do to a bloodbond who might have information?"

"Normally, most hunters won't hurt humans, even blood-bonds, but all bets are off now. They'll want information, and they won't show a lot of mercy getting it. Thank goddess Nissa got away."

"I, too, am relieved that Nissa is safe," Kaleo said, "but Nissa got away because Heather threw herself at the hunters, probably assuming they wouldn't bother with a bloodbond, and certainly knowing that I would expect her to protect Nissa in any way she could. If she is now in danger, it is your fault, and I expect your help to retrieve her."

Sarah closed her eyes and let herself go completely still, visualizing calm and centered attention.

By the time she opened her eyes again, she had come to a decision. There was one difference between this and all the deaths before. As Nikolas had pointed out, even if Sarah was dead by Vida standards, she wasn't *dead.* Her family would be horrified at the notion of a vampire—a monster—walking around in the skin of someone who had once been one of them. Vidas didn't believe that vampires could ever be good. They would be thinking not about *if* Sarah went bad, but *when,* and would consider it a mark of respect for who she had been to destroy what she now was.

"It isn't right of me to put you all in this much danger. Dominique called on the Rights, but what she really wants is me." There was a feeling that was almost one of freedom, of relief, as she said, "If I turn myself in—"

Shouting from the two brothers interrupted her chilled determination, but Kaleo's words were what cut through to her: "Don't be absurd."

"Once they have me, they'll release Heather."

"So?"

She had expected anything other than blunt indifference from Kaleo. He had seemed to want to rescue his bloodbond, but Sarah realized she had misjudged him.

"I'm sorry if you can't understand this," she snapped, "but even if her life doesn't matter to you, it matters to me. I won't let her be hurt, possibly even killed, on my behalf."

"On the contrary, Heather means a great deal to me," Kaleo argued, "and I have no intention of letting her be killed. But neither do I intend to let them have you."

"Why do you care?" Christine interrupted, fury in her voice. "Or is it just that you don't share your victims?"

Kaleo looked at her with a long, considering gaze before saying, "I think Sarah would object to being thought of as a victim."

"And her opinion matters so much to *you*," the human spat.

"Do you think, little girl, that the fact that she has been my enemy negates the fact that she has my blood?"

"Doesn't it?" Christine said challengingly, but more softly now.

The reminder that Sarah was in any way related to Kaleo was not welcome to her. Yes, he had changed Nissa, who had changed Nikolas, who had changed Kristopher, and so it was—distantly—his blood that now made Sarah a vampire. But she wasn't going to call him family.

Sarah was about to protest Kaleo's claiming her as any-thing, but he turned from her to Nikolas to say, "And speaking of blood, Sarah needs to feed."

The words jolted Sarah into immediacy.

"I'm fine," she said. She could function fine for now. Her eating habits were not the immediate issue.

"You are *not* fine." While Kaleo argued with her, she could tell that Nikolas and Kristopher were examining her closely. "I can see the bloodlust in your eyes."

"I fed a few hours ago."

"On Kristopher, I know," Kaleo replied dismissively. "It was enough to keep you alive, but it won't be enough to hold you long, not when you're this young and under stress. You need live blood to sustain you."

Sarah knew she was in trouble when Kristopher agreed, saying, "If you don't feed soon, willingly, then you'll feed in a frenzy, and you'll probably kill someone. You don't want that."

She wasn't ready. There was too much else going on. She hadn't had time to take in any of it or figure out what she wanted or needed to do. She was supposed to have been at SingleEarth, where they could teach her how vampires survived without hurting anyone, not with Nikolas and Kristopher, who for all their protectiveness were admitted killers. Kristopher hadn't killed for the past fifty years, but he had stopped in an effort to support Nissa, not because he'd had a change of heart. Sarah doubted he would keep to his new ways now that he was back with his brother.

And she *really* didn't want to have this conversation in front of Kaleo, who she still very much wanted to kill. Maybe the vampire blood didn't make a person evil, but it obviously hadn't made him *good*.

"The longer we bicker here, the more trouble we court," Kaleo said. "Sarah, deal with your own needs. We can't hold your hand right now. Nikolas, Kristopher, I advise you to warn your people. If Heather is a valid target, then any human who attends our circuits is probably in danger. There is no point in rescuing one while others are picked off. Once our people are safe, we can decide how to remove the threat itself."

He disappeared, leaving them with yet another subject she wasn't ready for. Nikolas and Kristopher turned to her, but what was she supposed to say? The threat Kaleo had referred to was Sarah's family and oldest friends. Her mother, her sister and her cousin Zachary were the last of the Vida witches. They would be joined by hunters from other lines, like Michael, who had been Sarah's best friend before Dominique had decided they were getting too close and put her foot down.

Sarah would have to be a monster to fight them—no, not just fight, but kill, since that was the only way to stop them.

Or was it? There had to be another way. She just didn't know what it was.

CHAPTER 5

SATURDAY, 6:37 A.M.

ZACHARY PUT HIS head down while Adia drove. His power had been wrapped up in the vampire's when the blood-bond had jumped at him, so it had been much harder to incapacitate the girl now in their backseat. He had done what was necessary, but was paying for it with a pounding head and a rolling stomach.

He looked up long enough to assure himself that she was completely out. Trapped in a moving vehicle with someone whose strength, speed and healing might be almost vampiric, and who probably wouldn't hesitate to leap out a door or fight for the steering wheel at eighty miles an hour, would be a bad time to make a mistake. It had been stupid of him not to track her as a threat in the first place.

When they got home, he could tell that Adia was trying to be careful, but the jerking motion the car made upon stopping still nearly made him heave. He shoved the nausea back, though, forcing it out of his frame of awareness as he pushed open the door and stood on legs that didn't want to hold him.

"Do you need help?" Adia asked.

"I can handle it." His mind was buzzing with a kind of white noise. The pain had pushed all coherent thoughts away, and for the moment, that was kind of nice despite the agony. It wasn't so intense that he couldn't do his job, though.

He checked around to make sure no neighbors had gone out for an early-morning walk before he lifted Heather onto his shoulder again and carried her toward the house, where Dominique was standing in the front doorway. She wasn't tapping her foot; such a display of impatience would be a shocking loss of control for the Vida matriarch. He couldn't have said what it was about her expression that made him certain she was watching him with frustration.

He just knew she was. He had always been able to sense her moods, ever since she had taken him in. He had always been able to recognize the times when she'd looked at him and seen his mother, or his sister, and wondered why he alone had survived and when the fatal flaw that had ended each of their lives would manifest in him.

He had hoped she would be sleeping, as she had said to Adia, but perhaps like the rest of them she was too restless. She must have stayed up to see what they would discover at SingleEarth.

"What's this?" Dominique asked as they approached.

"Kaleo's favorite bloodbond, I believe," Zachary answered. His voice was too loud, but he held himself from flinching or whispering. "Heather. We found Nissa, but then this one attacked us, and the vampire got away." Dominique's expression shifted; there was just the barest tightening between her brows. Zachary added, "She should be able to tell us a good deal. Kaleo is a major player in Nikolas's and Kristopher's circuit, and she will also probably be easier to persuade than a full-blooded vampire would be."

Reluctantly, Dominique nodded, as if his defensive babbling had in any way been new information to her.

"Bring her in. We should bind her before she wakes."

Fortunately, Dominique turned around too early to see him stumble on the steps. Adia caught his arm, steadying him.

"Are you okay?" she whispered.

He nodded, regretting the sharpness of the motion the instant he made it.

"Who else is here?" Adia asked as they followed Dominique to the kitchen. Zachary wondered at the question for a moment until Adia added, "I don't know all the cars in the driveway."

Zachary hadn't even looked. His senses were so dull at that moment he could probably have been run over by a truck without noticing.

"Jay Marinitch arrived a few minutes ago," Dominique answered. "Robert is also here."

Jay. Oh, joy. Zachary had known he would have to work with that hunter once the Rights were called, but he had hoped

Jay's flighty tendencies would keep him from showing up so promptly.

And then there was Robert Richards, the human would-be hunter. He lacked any recognizable discipline and had no formal training and was only of interest to Dominique because of his sister's connection to Nikolas. Christine Richards had been abducted by Nikolas the day before.

Neither Jay nor Robert would be much help in this hunt, and either could prove a hindrance. Robert's loyalties were downright questionable; Nikolas had apparently told him that Kaleo had tortured his sister and driven her mad, and had claimed he was taking Christine with him for her own good. Robert was just gullible enough to believe it.

"Zachary Vida goes out looking for a vampire, and comes back with a date."

The clear, almost musical voice belonged to Jay. His wit had never been to Zachary's taste, and now was no exception. Jay had the sense not to bait Michael, because he knew that the Arun witch would swing a punch at him, but Zachary didn't have that freedom.

Zachary set Heather down in one of the sturdy armchairs. Dominique had already gone to get rope and duct tape to bind her. Alone, the rope and tape together could not hold a bloodbond with Heather's strength, but they could be used as a base for magic that could dampen Heather's natural power and make the bonds more effective.

"Look here," Adia said, slipping something out of Heather's pocket as she helped arrange the bloodbond in the chair. "Cell phone!" She flipped open the phone and started hitting buttons. "Nothing in the address book . . . and it looks like she had the sense to clear incoming and outgoing calls before she attacked us . . . but there's one missed call."

"Anything familiar?" Zachary asked, though he didn't hold out much hope. There was a chance they could figure out the billing address for the cell phone if it was on a contract, but creatures who had been smart enough to survive being hunted for centuries tended not to be so easily caught.

"Looks like a local number," Adia answered. She turned and flipped open her laptop, which had been sitting on the kitchen counter, humming softly.

Robert, who had been staring at Heather since Zachary had brought her in, asked suddenly, "What is going *on*? Dominique called, and I showed up at six a.m. on a *Saturday* without asking a lot of questions. But if we're tying up random girls, I think I deserve to know why."

Zachary bit back a sharp retort. The human wasn't worth it. Past Robert, Dominique frowned, and only then did Zachary realize he had lifted a hand to rub his temple again.

"She's Kaleo's oldest, and by all indications favorite, blood-bond," he said, responding only to the last of Robert's demands. If Dominique had chosen to leave him in the dark about recent events, that was her call to make.

"Kaleo's?" Robert asked, brows rising. "Does that mean she's likely to help us out?"

"Don't. Bet. On. It." The growled words came from the girl on the chair as she shifted for the first time, testing her restraints. She rolled her head, making the joints in her neck and shoulders pop like cracking knuckles, and then looked up with blue-gray eyes.

Jay stood and slunk across the room to kneel, probably unwisely, in front of the bloodbond. Her feet were not tied to the chair, so Jay was risking a foot in the face, but if he wasn't bright enough to figure that out on his own, he didn't deserve a warning.

"A bloodbond's loyalty to her master tends to be fairly unwavering," Jay said, his words probably for Robert despite his holding Heather's gaze. "I will *hunt* as necessary, but I do not have the stomach for harsh interrogation. So unless Vida-kin have torture in their blood, I, too, wonder what we intend to do with this girl."

"We're not torturing anyone," Robert said, clearly horrified.

Zachary hoped it wouldn't come to that, but every Vida present knew they had less room to be idealistic than the Marinitch or the human.

"Found it," Adia said, still staring at the laptop screen. "It looks like that missed call was from an independent bookstore called Makeshift."

"If it's a store, anyone could have asked to use the phone," Zachary observed.

Dominique nodded. "We'll keep it in mind, but it's probably not worth—"

"I think you should check it out," Jay interrupted, still looking at Heather.

"While you're at it, could you pick up the book I ordered?" Heather asked sardonically.

Adia asked, almost too casually, "Do you know anything about this place, Jay?"

Zachary saw Dominique give Jay a wary look a moment before his mind caught up to what the other two Vidas had obviously already realized. Each line descended from Macht had its own skill set. The Vida line worked with raw power and could manipulate it in a variety of ways. The Arun line were faster and stronger than most witches and focused their training on offensive magic for fighting. The Smoke witches studied healing. Each Marinitch chose how to focus his abilities; some became hunters, some were healers, and some were closer to oracles or adjudicators. The Marinitch line was talented in empathy, bordering in some cases on telepathy.

Most hunters did not develop that skill; it was not beneficial to feel too much of what their prey experienced. Jay was apparently an exception.

He shrugged in response to Adia's question. "Nothing specific," he said.

Heather suddenly looked at Jay sharply, perhaps deducing the reason for his intent stare. At last she attempted the savage kick Zachary had predicted. Jay dodged handily.

"I'm going to check it out," Adia said. "The rest of you should stay here with our 'guest.'"

Dominique broke in: "I spoke to one of my informants shortly before you returned. He says he might know something, and asked me to meet him in the city."

Adia nodded, obviously not comfortable questioning her mother for more details. "If you think he's worth meeting, then we'll manage without you until you're back." To Zachary, she said, "You're in charge while we're both gone. Michael should be back soon to join you. You can catch him up. I imagine Kaleo will come for his property sooner rather than later."

Zachary nodded, acknowledging and assenting to her commands. Adia had a natural air of authority and confidence. He was happy to follow her lead.

Unfortunately, once she and Dominique were gone, he was alone with the Marinitch telepath, the human and the tied-up bloodbond.

"Anyone up for a round of go fish?" Jay asked after looking around the room. It was the kind of idiocy Zachary expected from him. Did it really even deserve an answer?

There was silence for the space of a few heartbeats, and then Heather pointed out, "I don't have a hand for the cards."

Robert said, "I guess I appreciate your calling me in if you're hunting Kaleo, but is this your entire plan? We're just going to hang out until an angry, thousands-of-years-old vampire shows up to try to kill us all?"

"Do you think we should rent a video?" Jay suggested, in his usual cavalier fashion.

"I'm going to take a nap on the couch," Zachary said. He had to get away from these three for a few minutes, and to lie down before he threw up.

Taunting and jokes aside, Jay paused to ask, "Are you all right?"

He didn't want to answer. Worse, he was worried he didn't *need* to answer. How much could Jay see, just looking at him? Zachary worked too hard to keep his external Vida poise to let some birdbrained Marinitch see what was inside.

"Don't worry," he said, putting up the same mental walls he would use to try to keep a vampire out of his thoughts, and speaking as if he assumed that Jay was asking about the plan and not his physical or mental condition. "The house is warded, so any vampire who plans to come for Heather will have to enter like a human, instead of appearing wherever he wants. If Kaleo shows, I'll be able to join the fight in plenty of time."

Jay nodded and waved him off.

He lay down. Strict training of his body allowed him to fall asleep almost instantly, but that sleep was far from restful. Dominique's earlier words had stirred up horrors that he normally tried to forget. It didn't take vampirism for sleep to recall a five-year-old child's nightmares come true.

He was just old enough to understand: Mama had gone mad. Someone had told her something bad, and she had gone wild. She had screamed and shrieked and cried in a way he hadn't thought Vidas even could. Then she had stormed out. Hours later, he had realized he was alone in the house. His older sister had already been missing for a week. His little brother had gone out the door after Mama.

No one came home.

As the day turned into night, he went through the cabinets to try to find something to eat. He went to bed when it got dark. He couldn't sleep.

He turned on every light in the house in an attempt to banish the shadows, and then he turned them off, because a Vida shouldn't be afraid of the dark.

He turned just one back on.

He fell asleep only when the dawn came, and woke because he was hungry. He scavenged for breakfast, the way he had done before. Someone had to come home soon.

When someone finally did, it wasn't Mama, but Jacqueline's friend Dominique. She brought him to her house and gave him dinner and then told him she was going back out to look for the rest of his family.

"Take care of the baby while I'm gone," she added.

He nodded solemnly. After Dominique left, he went into the nursery. She had taught him how to hold and feed and change a baby when he had visited before with his mother, but right then Adianna was sleeping, so he just sat next to the crib and listened to her breathe. He would protect her until everyone came home.

CHAPTER 6

SATURDAY, 6:38 A.M.

"SARAH—"

Sarah knew what Nikolas was going to say, and interrupted with "I won't kill my own family."

"And if it comes down to a choice between them and us?" he asked.

Kristopher tensed, his arms protective around Sarah. "We don't have to discuss this now. Much as I hate to say it, Kaleo is right. We need to talk to our people."

"Can I call Robert?" Christine's soft voice cut through the vampires' anxiety.

"I sent Robert to my mother for training, when I first learned he had been hunting," Sarah said with a wince. "She'll be watching him."

"We have some disposable cell phones," Kristopher said. "You can help Christine figure out what she can safely say."

Sarah was about to reject the idea again, but then she hesitated. Facing Kaleo the way Christine had was incredibly brave, considering her previous experiences with him. The seemingly frail human had been ripped from her own life as surely as Sarah had been, and this was the one comfort she asked.

Sarah realized, suddenly, that part of the sympathy she was feeling wasn't hers. She was picking up on Kristopher's thoughts again. She had forgotten to shield against him, and he had no ability to mask his mind.

She made an effort to block him out, but the damage—if that was what it was—had already been done. She could not be as cold and practical toward Christine as she wished to be.

She nodded. "We'll just have to be careful."

"Good," Nikolas said. "Meanwhile, Kristopher and I should go and speak to our people. They need to know the situation."

Sarah nodded, wondering with frustration, *When can we kill Kaleo?*

There. That was her cold practicality coming back to the surface. She wanted him *gone,* and making vampires gone was a task she knew how to handle. The ancient Roman had come to them this time looking for help to save one of his people, but that didn't negate his history of destroying anything and anyone who got in his way.

She must have projected the thought, because the brothers responded to it. Kristopher nodded to Nikolas, who waited with Christine while Kristopher pulled Sarah into the next room. In the past Sarah had been able, with effort, to communicate silently with Adianna, because they were close and they had often mingled powers for a hunt, but full-blown vampiric telepathy was a talent she would need some time to get used to.

"Killing him would kill Christine," Kristopher reminded Sarah, his voice every bit as bitter as she felt. Killing a bloodbond's master was almost always fatal to the bond, as the vampire's death was felt by the bonded human. The shock too often caused the body simply to shut down.

"I could protect her," Sarah said. "It will take me a while to get the hang of using my magic again, now that it's been changed by mixing it with vampiric powers, but I can feel it and I know it's not just *gone*. I don't know any magic that can break a bloodbond, but with effort, I should be able to block Christine's connection to Kaleo long enough that she wouldn't feel his death."

Kristopher paused to consider, but finally shook his head. "Kaleo already knows what thin ice he's on; that's why he didn't dispute our claim on Christine when we insisted on bringing her to stay with us. Nikolas and I would love an excuse to challenge him, but to do so now, especially when our actions have put his people in so much danger, would be seen by others of our kind as unprovoked."

"I find myself hard-pressed to care about the opinions of other vampires," Sarah said. "And even Nikolas said he would kill him. He said it to Christine."

"And you've never said anything in a moment of anger that you couldn't follow through with?" She didn't know how to respond to that, but a moment later, Kristopher spared her the need. He ran a hand through his long hair, frustrated, as he said under his breath, "Of course not. Vida control. You never say anything you don't mean, right?" He sighed and added, "I admire your self-discipline. It's *not* a trait most of our line shares, which is why we tend to hold to certain understandings, including that we don't kill each other over personal vendettas. If we did, we really would be the animals the hunters see us as . . . except there wouldn't be any hunters, because we would have killed ourselves off long ago."

Sarah was stunned, both by the bitterness in Kristopher's tone and the notion of such "certain understandings." She wasn't fully convinced that Kaleo wouldn't someday need killing, but she would hold her tongue on the subject, at least until the current crisis was dealt with.

Nikolas returned, expression somber. "Christine is activating one of the phones. It looks like it might take a while. Are we going to help Kaleo?"

"Will Heather help the hunters?" Sarah asked. Nikolas and Kristopher both shook their heads without even needing to consider. "Then they'll hurt her. She's old enough, and close enough to Kaleo, that if they decide she's useless, they might even kill her to weaken him."

"And we'll risk our necks rescuing her in order to help that bastard." Nikolas sighed. "Sarah, help Christine make her call, but get away from her before . . . Just get away from her."

"I'm not sure she should be alone right now," Sarah said.

"We won't be long," Nikolas said. "Trust me, Sarah. You don't know what a newly made vampire's hunger can be like."

"We'll help you feed safely as soon as we get the word out about the Rights," Kristopher said. "For now, be careful." He bent his head to kiss her, and whispered, "I love you," against her lips.

The brief touch of lips to lips should have been comforting, but for some reason it gave her chills. How many times had Kristopher said he loved her? She had never said it back to him. Should she?

Kristopher paused, as if hoping for a response, but then drew away. She didn't dare look at his mind; she didn't want to know if he was disappointed or relieved.

She felt numb.

The brothers both left, and Sarah sighed as some of the hard questions were deferred. She went to check on Christine, who was still struggling to activate the cell phone.

The tears on Christine's face made Sarah freeze in the doorway and think, *I don't know how to handle this.*

While Sarah tried to figure out what to say, Christine abruptly threw the phone across the room with a frustrated shriek. "Why do people have to be so *stupid?*" she cried as the phone broke through one of the windowpanes.

She stood up, and Sarah's first instinct was to tell her to sit down, shut up and *cope.* If anyone had a right to hysterics, it was Sarah, right? But Sarah was a daughter of Vida, and she wasn't allowed such a luxury, even now. It didn't matter that the sister who had once studied Vida law beside her was now using it to remove all barriers to killing her.

She found herself staring at the shards of glass hanging loosely in the shattered window. She wanted to convince herself that even if Dominique had called the Rights of Kin, Adia would never follow them, but no matter what Sarah wanted, that was too selfish a thought to contemplate. There weren't that many Vidas left. Adia couldn't throw it all away.

Sarah was standing there, immobile, when Christine flung herself into Sarah's arms and began to weep, her sobs almost as loud as the heartbeat that suddenly seemed to ricochet through Sarah's bones. She could feel Christine's pulse everywhere they touched as Christine shrieked, "I'm so . . . so . . . tired of being *helpless*!"

Sarah shut her eyes, trying to block out the sensation of the human's pulse and the scent of her skin.

"Robert tried to protect me. You protected me from Kaleo even though it meant trusting Nikolas. Nikolas and Kristopher try to protect me now, and I'm grateful and I *do* feel better, but I'm—" She broke off with a hiccup. "I'm an idiot. I'm sorry, Sarah, I'm so—" She choked back another sob, struggling to control herself, as she pulled herself back. At the same time, Sarah regained her own control, so she could meet Christine's eye without tasting the human's heartbeat on her tongue. "I'm so selfish. This has to be so hard for you. I wish, for once, that I could be someone who could fight, who could *help*, instead of someone you need to protect."

Sarah didn't think. She wasn't good at giving emotional comfort, but there was one thing she knew, and knew well, that she could use to help Christine. She asked, "Do you want me to teach you how to fight?"

Christine looked up slowly, seeming bewildered by the offer. "What?"

"You said you felt helpless," Sarah said. "I can teach you how to do things like protect yourself, and the people around you."

Christine gave her an odd look, partly of longing and partly of skepticism. Sarah expected her to say something denigrating her own potential as a fighter. Instead, she said, "Umm . . . I don't know how to put this, really, but . . . your family's methods for teaching fighting are kind of . . ." She trailed off, considered for a moment and then concluded with "cold."

Cold. That was one word for it. Sarah flexed her hand as the memory of her mother's reaction to her father's death passed through her mind again.

Nikolas and Kristopher had told her to get away from Christine because they worried Sarah would lose control, but neither of them understood what it was to be a Vida. She had been trained to ignore pain, and cold, and hunger. The moment of hyperawareness earlier had been no different, really. Self-control and discipline were at the heart of a Vida's training, because they meant a hunter could continue to fight no matter what happened.

A Vida did not give up, or make deals, or compromise, or flinch even when death seemed to be the only alternative. Their line had survived intact for tens of thousands of years by obeying that mandate. Dominique probably wasn't even as strict as some of her ancestors. At least Sarah had been allowed to attend public school and, to an extent, fraternize with hunters of a less-pedigreed birth.

On the other hand, if Dominique had been as harsh as Vidas had been historically, Sarah might not be in this mess.

"You don't have to follow Vida philosophy to learn some basic self-defense," Sarah said to Christine, keeping her "what if" thoughts to herself. "It's helpful to have some concept of focus and control, but most hunters don't go to the lengths my line does . . . did. Look at Nikolas and Kristopher. They fight well, especially when they're together."

Again, the words brought an unpleasant memory to mind. Sarah knew how well the two of them fought, and how cooperatively they worked in a fight, because that had been how she had lost.

Every hunter knew that the day would come when she was too slow, but most never needed to reflect on it afterward. They certainly did not wake up in the arms of the one who had taken them down.

"Anyway," she said. "I can teach you whatever you want to learn, even if it's just how to throw a punch or get out of a hold."

Christine nodded. "I think I would like that," she said. "It's finally getting through my mind that I could be around a *long* time, and I don't want to be a victim forever. Some of the blood-bonds I've met are like that. They just expect Nikolas to take care of everything. I want to scream at them, '*Who's taking care of him?*'"

Sarah smiled. "You know," she said wryly, "if you weren't in love with a vampire, you would probably make a good hunter. You have a strong instinct to protect people."

"Back at you, sister," Christine quipped. "We're in the same boat, maybe for eternity. So teach me something!"

Christine used it casually, but that word, *sister,* threw Sarah off balance. Where was Sarah's real sister now? Was she stalking innocents like Christine to get to Nikolas and Kristopher? Was she moving ever closer to checkmate, when Sarah would have to decide whether to stand with her birth kin or her blood kin?

Unsettled, she said, "I didn't really mean right *now*. What about calling Robert?"

Christine took a breath and dropped her gaze before saying, "Yeah, like I didn't see your face when I first asked. And you're right. Robert thinks your family is the good guys. I *want* to talk to him, but it would only get him into trouble. After this is sorted out, I'll call him, but until then I need to do *something*. C'mon. What else do you have to do tonight?"

Christine's heartbeat had already been fast because of her anxiety, but now her scent changed. Sarah wasn't sure how she recognized the difference, using a sense so new, but she could tell that Christine's fear dropped. The tangy spice of adrenaline filled the air. Her face flushed.

"What?" Christine asked.

"Hmm?"

Christine frowned. "Never mind, I guess. You looked like you were going to say something."

Sarah nodded, but she realized she could barely hear the words Christine was saying. The sound rising above all others in her ears was the *whoosh-whoosh* of blood racing through a hundred thousand miles of arteries, veins and capillaries. She realized that if she looked closely enough, she could see the beat not just at the pulse points, but across the surface of Christine's skin. It flickered like a fluorescent light.

And now there was fear in the air.

"Sarah?" Christine asked nervously.

The word—a name, so powerful that many ancient peoples had kept theirs forever secret from all but those closest to them—was just enough to let Sarah pull back a little and realize the tone her thoughts had taken.

Even once she was aware of it, she couldn't stop *looking*. She fought the instinct to move closer. She forced herself to take a step backward instead, but hellishly, contrary to any common sense, Christine responded by moving closer and reaching out as if she intended to touch Sarah, possibly to offer comfort but . . . *insanity!*

She had to get out of there.

She had been so confident about her self-control, so *arrogant,* she had forgotten something she had learned every day of her life: how "good" a person a vampire was, or tried to be, ceased to matter when the vampiric blood took over. There was a monster inside, and it would use the body it inhabited to do what it wanted. Sarah might think she was in control at that moment, but the blood inside her now would be with her the rest of her existence, just waiting for her to slip up.

Eventually, inevitably, she would. A moment would come when she was too weak to stop herself, and when that moment was done, she would be left with an innocent corpse in her arms.

She pulled away from Christine. She had to get somewhere safe . . . where *she* was safe . . . no, where she would be made safe. Her self-control would only get worse from here on out.

She had to do this while she still could, before she did something terrible.

She went home.

CHAPTER 7

SATURDAY, 7:05 A.M.

ZACHARY WOKE SHAKING, sweating and scared. He didn't remember the dreams that had forced him from sleep with his heart pounding and the sharp tang of adrenaline on his tongue, and for that he was grateful. Sometimes he *did* remember, and those mornings were never easy.

He didn't get up immediately, didn't even open his eyes. Instead, he lay perfectly still, barely breathing, until the flush of fight-or-flight passed. He realized his jaw was clenched, as if he had been bracing against pain and struggling not to scream.

He tossed onto his stomach, curling his arms under his head until his right hand found the hilt of his knife sheathed on his left wrist, like a child grasping a teddy bear for comfort.

He wished he could sleep for another hour. Maybe he would have a good dream.

Or maybe another nightmare.

What dragged him up was not fear of sleeping demons, but the knowledge that Dominique wouldn't approve of his oversleeping when there was work to do.

By the time he opened his eyes, he was perfectly composed, enough that even Dominique wouldn't have recognized the terror that had filled him only a minute before.

He glanced at the clock; he had slept for twenty-four minutes, just enough to revive him and get rid of the headache.

He ducked briefly into the kitchen, where he found Michael, Jay and Robert. Michael was bent over a SingleEarth-published book about shapeshifter physiology. Jay was looking through the window with a pair of small binoculars, probably birdwatching. Robert was staring at Heather, who was either sleeping or unconscious. Maybe someone had finally gotten fed up with her.

Jay replied to what Zachary was about to ask before Zachary could say anything out loud. "We're fine here. Dominique just called. She'll be back in a minute, probably in a foul mood, since she says her informant stood her up, but you should have some time to clean up first."

Robert looked confused when Jay first spoke, and then startled to find another hunter standing over his shoulder. Michael glanced up and then returned to his book without uttering a word.

"I'll do that, then," Zachary said. He had forgotten to shield his thoughts when approaching the kitchen. He wouldn't make that mistake again. He would, however, take Jay's advice. The shirt he was wearing still had blood on it from Heather's X-Acto attack.

He had only a couple of outfits in this house—Dominique had asked him to stay here while they tracked Sarah, and he hadn't brought many of his belongings—but that was fine, because to Zachary Vida, *dressed* could mean any clothing plus two things: a weapon and a woven silver chain with a white-gold pendant in the figure-eight symbol for eternity. The chain was his only remaining memento of his mother. The pendant had been a gift from another woman.

Dominique didn't know either one existed, as both were always hidden by his undershirt, which was under the harness that held his primary knife at the small of his back.

Once fully dressed, he returned to the kitchen; he walked in just in time to see Dominique backhand Heather. Robert grabbed the witch's arm and dragged her away from the blood-bond, earning a cold warning expression that made even the foolhardy human take a step back.

"This isn't going to help anything," Robert protested. "She already hates us. Beating her up isn't going to make her like us more."

"And you claim to be the good guys," Heather snapped.

The expression on Dominique's face was enough to make Zachary hesitate in the doorway. Though few other people would have noticed, Zachary could see the tension at the edges of her eyes and lips.

He would never ask about it, but he *did* wonder: Was there part of Dominique that was weakened by the loss of her daughter? Was there anywhere in her heart where she blamed herself? Could Dominique Vida feel regret, or was she just frustrated by the delay in catching her current prey?

Zachary understood impatience. When he had been eight, he had spent as many hours walking the colicky Sarah as he had training. He had warmed bottles at three in the morning and sung her to sleep when her father wasn't home to do so. He had held her hands as she'd learned to walk, and grinned in a very un-Vida fashion as she'd learned her first fighting forms. Now every minute that passed was a minute when he failed her and let her dead body be violated.

He tried to strike the thoughts from his mind. That way lay the same kind of madness of grief that had gripped his mother after Jacqueline was taken, and a kind of shame he had no desire to share with the Marinitch next to him.

Perhaps too abruptly, he asked, "Jay, isn't this what *you're* here for?"

As frail as Heather looked, Zachary did not doubt that she would be willing to kill every one of them if given a chance. And she had certainly experienced worse abuse at Kaleo's hands than Dominique was unleashing now—which meant Robert was right: this was a useless way of getting her to talk. Why wasn't the damned telepath doing his job?

Jay turned in his seat to answer the question, naked gratitude on his face as he looked away from Dominique. "This one has been around vampires for a couple centuries, I'd guess. She knows how to obscure her thoughts. Anything you could do to her that is severe enough to disrupt her concentration would cause too much distress for me to read her past it."

Dominique turned from the bond, just slowly enough to reveal that she was not satisfied with the single blow.

At that moment, however, Heather tossed her head. "You want me to talk? I could tell you things to give you nightmares. Worse, maybe I could give you *happy* dreams. Would you like to know what it's like when one of them takes you? When you're in their arms and they bare your throat and drink?"

Zachary stood very still and fought to keep his mind blank. *Blank.* Not filled with the images the bloodbond's words evoked. Yet she continued.

"I've been told that Kendra's line is the best at it, though naturally I've never experienced anything else. All I know is that *nothing* you can do to me here matters for more than a moment. I've had three hundred years, and even if you kill me today, I will always have something you will *never* have: peace. You call me a victim, but I think maybe I am the only one in this room who isn't. Look in my head if you want to," she said, challenging Jay. "I have seen hundreds of humans pass through, willing to die, willing to give up everything, just to experience that bliss. And not just humans. The Vida line isn't immune, is it?"

Zachary had been staring, hypnotized, so it took him by surprise when Dominique hit the bloodbond again, this time hard enough to rock her head back and unfocus her eyes.

Heather spat blood onto the floor before saying, "Sarah liked it enough to die for it."

Michael was apparently the only sensible person left in the room. He tore off another strip of duct tape and slapped it over Heather's bruised mouth.

"I'm going out," Dominique announced.

No one questioned her as she left. Dominique's self-control and composure might be perfect, but even she had to be disturbed by such an accusation regarding one of her blood. Of course she would want to get away.

"Sarah's dead?" Robert asked in the silence that followed. No one had told him *why* he had been called to Dominique's house. And apparently, no one was in the mood to answer him now.

Zachary looked around, trying to focus on his surroundings and not on his thoughts. He found Jay sitting in the corner, not quite out of the room but as far from Heather as he could get without truly fleeing. Whatever he had seen in Heather's mind in those moments had shut him down.

"We should just get rid of her," Michael said. "As long as we are guarding her, we are not out hunting Nikolas and Kristopher, and any secure locations she knows about will be empty long before we pry the information out of her."

"I thought this was a trap for Kaleo," Robert said weakly. "Sarah can't be dead. Heather was messing with us, wasn't she?"

"This being a trap assumes the mass-murdering sadist cares enough about this particular human to risk his hide," Michael said, ignoring the human, as they all were. "We have more important prey to track."

"*She* absolutely believes that he will come," Jay said softly as he pushed himself to his feet. "Whether or not she is right, I do not know."

"Like it or not, she's one of our only leads," Zachary said. "I *do* believe Kaleo will come for her, and even if he doesn't lead us to our targets, removing him will make hunting them easier. We also need her in case Adia's trip to the bookstore doesn't pan out. After she gets home, she can decide what we do with this one."

"'This one'?" Jay echoed. "You're trying so hard to distance yourself from her mentally, you can't even stand to see her as human, can you?"

"She barely *is* human," Michael replied. "After a couple hundred years, a bloodbond gets to be a lot more like a vampire. They get strong, and fast, and some of them even feel the bloodlust. If we give her a chance, she will kill us all."

"Not all bloodbonds—"

"Shut *up*, Robert," Zachary snapped.

"Did Nikolas kill Sarah?" Robert asked, gaze level and nearly empty.

Zachary nodded.

"He's got my sister," Robert said. "I thought . . . I thought she was safe with him."

"The situation isn't quite as clear-cut as it seems," Jay said.

"Shut up, Marinitch," Michael advised. "We don't need you playing shrink with us."

"I'm just trying to—"

Michael stood abruptly, his chair clattering to the floor behind him as he grabbed Jay by the shirtfront and shoved him back against the wall. "Trying to *what*?" the Arun said, challenging him. "Make us realize how hard this is? Trust me, we've got that covered. Zachary and I have known Sarah all her life. We trained with her and fought with her. We have watched each other's backs in fights none of us would have survived on our own. You and Sarah have barely even been introduced. You think this is hard? You have no idea."

He slammed a fist into the wall only inches from Jay's head, as if his self-control was sufficient to keep him from hitting the other witch, but not enough to keep him from needing to lash out. Jay shut his eyes as plaster shattered, and then Michael dropped him, the argument abruptly forgotten as his attention shifted. It took Zachary a moment longer, but then he, too, sensed what had silenced Michael.

The power was faint, even with the wards around the house acting like an antenna. The vampire was lingering at least a block away, not coming closer at that moment, but near enough that they could all feel her there.

Her. Not Kaleo. The power Zachary could sense was not nearly enough for the ancient Roman to be approaching.

Was it Sarah? Could things be so convenient?

It had to be a trap. He stretched his awareness, trying to find more of her kind but knowing it was pointless, since they could appear at any time with no warning. Did she think she could trick them into trusting her and letting down their guard?

Had she come to turn herself in?

He squashed the thought. The vampiric animal always sought survival. He had to brace himself, because he knew that the vampire outside would look like Sarah, and sound like Sarah. But it wouldn't *be* Sarah; it would be the thing that had killed her.

Maybe, it occurred to him, Kaleo had threatened her. Zachary hadn't considered that obvious possibility before, that the other vampires might have turned on her. The twins were very protective of their sister, and the hunters had threatened her. Kaleo was incredibly possessive of the individuals he considered *his*. Maybe they had sent their newest fledgling here as a sacrifice to appease the hunters.

Or it could be a trap.

CHAPTER 8

GIVEN THE HOUR at which Heather had received her phone call, Adia was not entirely surprised to find that the Makeshift bookstore was connected to a twenty-four-hour coffee shop. The bookstore itself was closed, but the café had its own door to the street.

Adia damped down her witch aura as she stepped out of the car, and as she crossed the threshold, she mentally donned a mask. Who should she be today? A college student, probably, on the way home from an all-night study session at a friend's house, and not quite ready to go back to her roommate. She was social and friendly, confident, but possibly a little naïve about the real world.

In theory, the Vida line was the most famous line of vampire hunters in history and should therefore be the most recognizable. In reality, especially in this generation, there were a lot of blond girls with blue eyes in the world. It meant she could be anyone she needed to be, and while she was lost in that role, she didn't need to think about anything more than the immediate objective. The person she chose to be didn't need to have a sister, or a grim duty to fulfill.

She knew her cheeks would be pink from having driven the last mile with the window down. She let herself shiver as she came in from the cold.

At seven-thirty in the morning on a Saturday, the atmosphere was subdued. The two young girls seated at a back-corner booth, eating sweet sticky pastries, both felt like bloodbonds, but there was also an older woman, reading the *Boston Globe* and sipping coffee, who probably had no idea that the man behind the counter was a vampire.

That bloodsucker smiled at Adia, his expression tired but friendly.

"I'm sorry, but if you're looking for a place to stay, you're out of luck."

The way he had tossed out that information to a complete stranger suggested that enough people had been bothering him for help that he was getting fed up with it. That was only likely to be the case if individuals hiding from the Rights of Kin were coming to him, which would only happen if he was connected to Nikolas and Kristopher.

She flashed her own best long-day smile and said, "Actually, I was looking for a cup of coffee. Am I in the wrong place?"

His expression shifted as he focused his attention, seeming to draw himself together. "Sorry," he said. "Yes, of course, coffee right away. How do you take it?"

She glanced at the menu behind the counter, trying to determine what kind of place she was in. Keeping to her pretense, she said, "I don't care. Something sweet, with a lot of caffeine and a *lot* of sugar."

"Starting the day with a kick, I see," the vampire joked with her as he turned to the espresso machine.

"I'm normally more of a night person," she answered. "I got up early to drive a friend to work, and have to hide from my roommate so she won't drag me to Zumba."

He chuckled. She could almost see the gears turning in his head. It was past dawn, the hour when decent vampires normally wanted to sleep, and she could tell he hadn't had a chance to feed the night before. Here was a cute girl who no one expected home soon, who was willing to chat with strangers . . . and who, therefore, could probably be persuaded to go somewhere more private. He handed her the coffee, and the smile he turned on her was considerably warmer than the first one had been.

"I know what you mean," he said. "My roommates have guests over at all sorts of crazy hours. Here's your coffee, on the house. My shift's pretty much—" He cut off, a moment after Adia sensed the aura of the bloodbond who had just walked up behind her. "Matt, it isn't often you darken my door. Is something wrong?"

Adia turned, trying to make it look casual. She wasn't sure

whose bloodbond she was facing, but knew that the olive-skinned "young" man was decades older than he appeared. Bloodbonded humans, like vampires, didn't age.

Matt lifted a hand to brush sandy brown hair back from his face, and the cuff of his long sleeve pulled back just enough for Adia to see the edge of a scar. *Nikolas's marks*—a rose, a strand of ivy and Nikolas's name. She was sure of it. Pure vanity made the vampire carve his symbols into the flesh of his victims. It also made them easy to identify.

Cold affected bloodbonds less than pure humans, so most of Nikolas's bloodbonds wore their arms bare in any weather, no matter how much harassment it earned them from normal humans. Someone must have warned this one to cover up.

"Can I talk to you in private for a moment?"

The vampire looked from Adia to the bloodbond who had just walked in, probably torn between some sense of obligation and the prospect of a free meal. Adia debated interrupting to offer her name or phone number, but decided that would be too blatant.

She took the coffee and sought a quiet table in the back of the room, where she pulled out a science fiction novel she kept in her purse for when she needed an excuse. It would have been nice to eavesdrop on the two at the counter, but the vampire brought Matt into the back room, leaving a BE RIGHT BACK sign by the register. Adia supposed he didn't care what customers he might miss.

Adia took the opportunity to scan the coffee shop over the pages of her book. This time of year, long sleeves weren't exactly noteworthy, so there was no way to know if the other bonds in the room belonged to Nikolas. The real question was, why had someone called Heather from here? The phone was behind the counter, but customers might be allowed to use it. Anyone could have called; the phone itself wouldn't give her anything more. Fortunately, every hunter knew that the friend of her enemy made a useful friend, and it looked like the local vampire might be a very good friend.

After about two minutes secluded in the back room with Matt, he returned to the café, nodded to a sleepy-looking human to man the counter and then slid into the seat across from Adia.

"What I was about to say was my shift is up," he said. "I would ask if you'd like to get a cup of coffee, but I seem to have already provided that." When she chuckled, he added, "My name's Jerome."

"Anna," she replied. "Was that one of your friends looking for a place to stay?"

"More like a friend of a vague acquaintance, who only shows up when he needs a favor," Jerome answered.

"Oh?" She wasn't expecting him to tell the truth to the human he thought she was, but most people included nuggets of reality in their lies. She could sift for those.

Before Jerome could answer, someone else—a girl this time, with no hint of a bloodbond that Adia could make out— tapped him on the shoulder.

Jerome sighed. "I think it's going to be one of those mornings," he said as he glanced up at the girl trying to get his attention and gave her a halfhearted glare. Jerome jotted down a couple of words on a napkin—an address, Adia was almost certain—and passed it off. Adia watched out of the corner of her eye as the human read the address, presumably memorized it, and tucked the napkin into a not-quite-empty coffee cup before she tossed them both into the trash. The liquid would destroy the writing, which kept people like Adia from stealing the napkin to get the address.

"You're popular," Adia observed.

"I'm more like an information center," he answered with a self-deprecating chuckle.

Adia glanced at the clock behind the counter and sighed dramatically. "I hate to caffeinate and run, but you seem pretty busy, and I should probably get home sometime."

Walking away was a gamble. She was betting on the reaction the person he was pretending to be would have to the person she was pretending to be. She couldn't take him on in a place this public, and she couldn't wander into the back room with him and become dinner. That meant she needed to leave but give him a reason to keep in touch after she left so she didn't lose her only contact.

"Anna." He said her name as she started to turn away.

She felt a brief moment of triumph, and then her cell phone rang. A wave of dread passed through her before she even saw Zachary's number on the screen.

"Sorry," she said to Jerome before she answered the phone. "Hey, Bill." To Jerome, she added, "My brother," just loudly enough that Zachary would hear it. He would know she was with someone with sensitive enough hearing to eavesdrop on anything he said on the phone. Someone who didn't know who or what she was.

Zachary's voice was light and perfectly cheerful as he said, "Good, I caught you. I never know what kind of hours you keep." He chuckled. "Mom wanted me to ask if you think you're going to be able to make it for Thanksgiving this year. It looks like Liz is planning to come home, and it would be great to have the whole family."

It was a struggle to keep herself composed in front of Jerome. Were his vampiric senses enough for him to hear the twist in her guts or feel the cold pit that developed in her stomach? Zachary was telling her that Sarah was there . . . or was possibly on her way.

"I'm not sure I can get off work in time to make it," she said. She was nearly an hour away from home, and she didn't have a vampire's ability to instantly transport from place to place. Even if she drove as fast as she very well knew her car could handle, it was likely to be over before she got home. "How definite is Liz?"

"She's going to hang out a little while, but I don't know yet if she'll actually be at dinner," he answered.

Sarah had to be near enough that Zachary could sense her, but she hadn't declared her intention. She could just be lurking, observing, looking at her once family or trying to see what kind of guard they had on Heather. She could be intending to turn herself over, and hadn't yet found the courage, or she could have come to try to fight.

"I want to be there," Adia said. "I'll do my best."

"I'll let her know," Zachary answered. "Take care of yourself. Get some sleep."

"You too," she answered.

They were all such liars.

"You don't look happy at the idea of going home," Jerome observed when Adia ended the call and tucked the phone into her pocket.

She hadn't expected him not to notice her obvious reaction to the news, so she had an answer ready. "I have a difficult relationship with my family."

"Don't we all?" Jerome answered with a laugh. "If you end up wanting turkey without the complications, the Makeshift hosts Thanksgiving for anyone who wants to show up." He went behind the counter for a few minutes, looked around and came back with a small flyer. "I just got these printed, and wasn't planning to put them out until this weekend, but you're welcome to one."

Vampire Thanksgiving.

That was sure to be a hoot.

"Thanks," she said. Strangely, her smile felt genuine. Thanksgiving at home normally meant pizza. Now, if she was looking for an easy kill and some pumpkin pie, she would have somewhere to go. "You know, I should get going, but how about you give me your number, and I'll give you a call sometime?" she asked. If Sarah was turning herself in, they probably wouldn't need the lead, but it would be stupid to break the connection before determining how useful it might be.

Jerome obliged, giving her a different number than the one that went directly to the shop. It looked like a cell phone exchange, but there were so many these days that it was always hard to tell.

"Call anytime," he said. "I tend to stay up late."

"Me too."

She managed to keep her heartbeat from ringing in her ears until she made it back to her car. While she had been inside, dawn had transformed into full day—one of those bitter mornings when the sky was so perfectly blue it was hard to believe that the wind could have such a bite to it. At least that meant there wouldn't be any morning joggers or bikers to get in her way as she pushed as much speed into the car as it could handle. She trusted her reflexes to keep her from a collision. Worst-case scenario, she could sweet-talk any cop, add a push of power and make a possible ticket disappear. There were more important things at stake.

Absently, she wondered why she felt such a need to hurry. Did she really *want* to get there in time? Was it selfish to hope in some ways that Zachary would do what she hadn't been able to and end all this before she even stepped through the door?

CHAPTER 9

SATURDAY, 7:31 A.M.

SARAH STOOD ACROSS the street from where she had once lived, well aware that the witches inside the house would sense her, but trying to get her thoughts and the scraping of the vampiric hunger under control enough to make a plan. The early-morning sun was a worse slap in the face than the winter wind. It illuminated a peaceful neighborhood, where some houses still boasted decorations not yet taken in from Halloween, and some were already prepared for Thanksgiving. A few brightly colored leaves still fluttered on the trees.

It was a pretty day to die.

For a little while, she had been too dazed to think past Nikolas's, Kristopher's and Kaleo's vehement responses to her statement that she had to turn herself in. She had let them wrap her up in their insistence that she had a right to go on, but she *didn't*. As a hunter she had accepted the possibility of her own death. She had never wanted to wake as a vampire. She didn't *want* to die, but she had no right to endanger so many others with her continued existence when her time had come and gone.

Her arrogance had almost gotten Christine hurt—or worse. She had to fix this mess before it was too late and she lost the will to do what needed to be done, and there was only one sure way to do that. Dominique had invoked the Rights of Kin because her daughter had been transformed into a vampire. She would declare satisfaction once she knew that her daughter was . . . at rest.

The only hitch was Heather. The bloodbond was already in Vida custody, and they were unlikely to give her up just because the Rights of Kin were dropped. However, Sarah was the more valuable target, which meant an exchange that would ensure Heather's safety once this was all over might be possible.

Unless the witches inside held to the law of never making deals with vampires.

Once she was certain she was reasonably well under control, she crossed the street. She was not surprised to see the front door open. Zachary stepped onto the front porch, and Sarah stopped on the sidewalk. They should have been somewhere in the old west, with tumbleweeds and a saloon to mosey into, not in peaceful suburbia, surrounded by rotting pumpkins and straw turkeys.

Zachary's expression was as impossible to read as ever. He wore a slight smile that she had seen often enough when they had hunted together to know it was meaningless, and had his hands tucked into his back pockets. The position looked casual, but Sarah knew that it meant he had a knife sheathed at the small of his back. The only reason he hadn't drawn it yet, she was sure, was the possibility of nosy neighbors peering out their windows. He would try to take the fight inside if he could.

His heartbeat was perfectly even. It wasn't like the flawless Zachary to lose control in such a silly situation as preparing to murder his cousin.

"I'm not here to fight," she said, lifting her voice enough that he would hear it, but hoping the words wouldn't travel to the neighbors. "I'm here to . . ." Her voice trailed off. Would it kill him to look *human* once in a while? She shook her head and reached for her knife, which she had strapped to her wrist. It was warm to the touch these days, even uncomfortably hot.

Zachary tensed slightly, one arm shifting as he went for his own blade, but when he realized she was undoing the straps that held the sheath in place, he returned to his prepared but relaxed posture.

She set the knife, still securely sheathed, on the grass.

"I came to return this, and to turn myself in," she said. The words were a little more tight, and a little louder, than she had intended, but she had never had Zachary's perfect control.

At least she didn't have to face Adia this way.

"All I want," she said, taking a step away from where she had left the knife, "is for Heather to go free before I turn myself in. She's human, just a bloodbond. Once you have me, you don't need her."

She could see somewhere in Zachary's glacier blue eyes the exact moment that he decided she was trying to play him.

"Turn yourself in, and I'll give you my word that she will be let free."

Sarah's laugh sounded a little like a snarl. "I grew *up* with you, Zachary! Trust me, damn you."

"*You* did not grow up with me. *Sarah* grew up with me," he replied. "Do we have a deal?"

"If I'm not Sarah to you, then I know for a fact that your word means nothing," she said. "If I'm just a vampire, then you can swear on your mother's grave and it's all meaningless."

Stalemate. There had to be a way to get past this.

Zachary had long been an enigma to her. She had hazy memories of his being around when she was young, but the one that stood out most in her mind was the resigned expression on his face as he watched Dominique bind her powers and set her broken fingers after her father's death. He had apologized to her later, though she had never been sure why.

Had they been closer before then? She remembered that he had moved out the next day, and that his visits after then had always been purely business, either to work on a hunt or to help her and Adia train. He had never played "nice" when training. She had liked that as a kid. It meant that by the time she was strong enough to beat him, she never doubted that she had done it fairly.

She moved closer. He couldn't hold her here as long as she stayed out of his reach. Zachary had the finest control over his raw magic and was able to do things with it that Sarah had never quite grasped, but for the past few years she had almost always been able to take him down in a plain old-fashioned physical fight. If he grabbed for her, she trusted herself to get out of his grip.

"Bring Heather to the door," she said. "Then we can decide our next step."

He nodded slowly and then glanced behind him. He didn't need to speak.

Robert and Michael escorted Heather onto the porch. Christine's brother looked pale and shaken. He stared at Sarah with first relief, then confusion and finally blatant horror. Michael's face was flushed, and his anxiety was clear in all his features. He refused to look in Sarah's direction, which was at least less of a stab in the gut than Zachary's calm and even gaze. Heather's expression was hard to read past the duct-tape gag. Her feet were free, but her hands were bound in some way behind her back.

Sarah took a few more steps forward. She trusted Robert and Michael more than she trusted Zachary, but Zachary was the one in charge.

"Robert, if you will walk Heather out to the street and untie her, I will go inside with Zachary and Michael."

Robert looked from Zachary to Sarah as if begging someone to stop this madness.

I'm trying to, Sarah thought in response.

Michael shadowed Robert and Heather until they were even with Sarah on the front walk.

"I didn't know," Robert said to Sarah. His gaze held confusion, guilt, fear and indecision. She recognized it because it was the same tangle of emotions she had felt not long before. *Whose side do I fight on?*

"It's okay," she replied. The human couldn't help her now, but he could be hurt if he tried. "Get Heather to safety. Don't worry about me."

She stepped back, giving them a clear path and keeping herself well away from any of the hunters. Once Robert was a fair distance away, she looked back at Zachary.

"Let's do this inside, shall we?" she asked.

He nodded.

She heard Michael swallow thickly as he leaned down to retrieve her knife from the ground. As Zachary turned back toward the house, Michael whispered, "Sarah—"

She interrupted. "I can't go on like this, Michael. I can't stand to have innocent people in danger because of me." She left him at her back as she ascended the front steps. "Dominique and Adianna aren't here?"

"Why do you ask?" was Zachary's response.

Maybe I just wanted to see if Dominique could look me in the eye and tell me I'm a monster, the way you can, Sarah thought.

Okay. She had done her duty. She had made sure Heather was safe. Robert was a good guy, in addition to his sister's being one of Kaleo's bloodbonds. He would make sure Heather was properly untied and knew which direction to go to get to safety.

The wards protecting the house from vampires seemed to scrape across her skin as she crossed the threshold.

"Hi, Sarah."

She looked up at the unexpected greeting, which came from a hunter she only vaguely knew, as they all reached the living room. She had seen Jay at major events, when all the lines gathered, but she wasn't certain they had been officially introduced.

"Hi," she replied.

"This is awkward," he said.

Michael giggled, the sound almost hysterical.

They were still all standing just out of striking distance from each other. She was pretty sure Michael and Jay had absolutely no intention of attacking her. Neither even looked inclined to draw a weapon. Zachary was probably waiting for a clear shot or a solid indication from her of whether she planned to fight.

She decided she was grateful that Zachary was the one there. She put her hands behind her back, clasping them together, sure that he wouldn't hesitate. He would make it quick, and she would never see in his eyes the betrayal she imagined she would have seen in Adia's.

The sound of shattering glass from the next room interrupted them an instant before she sensed Kristopher. Sarah instinctively fell back, unsure how to respond immediately. Michael's eyes widened, and a look of betrayal crossed his face as he set Sarah's knife down and drew his own. A hunter's magic was twined to his primary blade; Michael would risk the low likelihood of Sarah's retrieving the Vida knife, rather than try to fight with a weapon tied to someone else.

How dare Kristopher come here? Sarah thought. *Doesn't he know how hard this already is?*

Zachary said to the other hunters, "Check on it."

Jay and Michael obeyed instantly, any disagreement between the three men now forgotten in the face of a threat.

If Kristopher was here, was Nikolas? The hunger had made her too unfocused to sense clearly. Had Heather somehow called them? How could she have had time? If he was here alone, Michael and Jay would kill him. He didn't stand a chance. Those thoughts whipped through Sarah's mind, and she moved toward the kitchen, intending to cut off Michael and Jay, as she shouted mentally at Kristopher, *Get out of here!*

The answer that slapped her with its intensity was, unequivocally, *No!*

She didn't have time for anything more. Seeing her move, Zachary reacted; she barely managed to dodge the knife she should have known was coming.

They had fought countless times. They knew each other's weaknesses. His power was more of a danger to her now that she was a vampire; her strength and speed, however, were greater than they had been when she had been a witch.

On the other hand, she had one serious handicap: she didn't want to kill him. She wanted to incapacitate him *quickly,* without doing permanent damage. Even if she no longer agreed with everything she had been taught growing up, the world needed hunters—and she would never kill someone who had been her family. Zachary might have been able to sever the connections in his heart, but she didn't think she would ever be able to do the same.

It was very hard to be careful when she had been trained all her life to kill. She didn't dare try to reach her knife. A blade would only remind her body of deadly habits.

Behind Zachary, she saw two figures move past the doorway. She wasn't close enough or sufficiently focused to tell if it was Nikolas or Kristopher who Michael had just dragged through her line of sight, one arm around the vampire's neck as if in a stranglehold. It was impossible to tell from the glimpse if Michael had a knife in play, or if it had been lost, and she had no idea what Jay was doing.

In her moment of distraction, Zachary lunged. She dodged but not quite quickly enough; his knife tore a gash deep into her shoulder. The wound cut through the rose scar as if striking it out, and the poisonous magic in the blade sent agony down to her fingertips and then swirling toward her core.

She had been trained for many years to experience pain and push it out of her mind until she had the chance to deal with it. She had been taught to focus no matter what other stimuli were around.

Something went wrong.

The pain and anxiety and frustration and fear all mingled in the spot where her heart now sat silent and unused except by the parasite that gave her life, and suddenly she beheld the world through a haze. Her mind stopped tracking details and intentions, like protecting Kristopher without killing Zachary. She moved. They fought in a whirlwind. When Jay tried to join on Zachary's side, she managed to get just enough of a grip on his arm to throw him into the wall, hard. She paid only enough attention to see someone else engage him before returning her focus to the more dangerous witch.

Zachary got past her guard. She twisted just enough for the knife to miss her heart, but it cut into her stomach and sliced upward. Her eyes widened with shock, her body frozen for the moment with the pain. For the first time, Zachary's eyes met hers, and in them she saw regret.

"I'm sorry, Cousin," he whispered.

He hesitated.

She didn't.

Snarling, mindless beyond the pain and the predator screaming in her head, she grabbed his wrist and squeezed until she felt it splinter. He shuddered, but he was a Vida. He didn't cry out.

He had what she needed. She locked her prey's wrists together in one hand, so slight and delicate but possessing a vampire's terrible strength, and then with the other hand she pinned him in place and leaned his head to the side.

As if sensing his defeat, he went limp. In that last second, he didn't fight her at all.

Warmth where she had been cold. Peaceful satisfaction where there had been gnawing hunger. She wasn't fighting anymore. She was feeding, and the predator within her purred with triumph.

The voice seemed very far away, even though she knew it was screaming: *"Sarah!"*

She growled without lifting herself away from her prey.

"Sarah, you have to let him go," the voice pleaded. Hands tried to pull her back. *"Sarah, he's your cousin. You won't be able to live with yourself if you kill him."*

CHAPTER 10

ZACHARY WAS AWARE of nothing beyond the waves of need and satisfaction so deep they felt like love. His mind wandered, his memories skipping through events that he and Sarah had both experienced—moments of exhilaration, when they had fought together and known they were on top of the world.

At least, he thought, *I'll be dying with family.*

When it stopped, he wanted to weep.

"You take her," a familiar voice said. "Your brother needs her help. I will take care of this one."

"Don't kill him," another voice said. "We came here to stop Sarah from doing something stupid, not to destroy everyone she once called family."

"I won't kill him. I'll even call a healer, once the three of you are gone. Now *go!*"

Zachary managed to open his eyes just in time to feel himself lifted. He couldn't raise a hand to defend himself, much less to shove the vampire carrying him away.

He couldn't even raise any mental shields, so when the vampire looked at him and said, "Get some rest," with a tiny nudge of power to go along with the command, Zachary fell into deep black sleep.

He woke on the couch with Caryn Smoke leaning over him, putting stitches into his side where Sarah had shoved his own knife back at him. It looked like she had already wrapped his wrist with a compression bandage. It had felt like Sarah had fractured his wrist, but it must have been minor enough for Caryn to mostly heal it before he woke.

"Don't try to sit up yet," she said, tying off the last stitch and taping a bandage over it. "There's juice on the end table. You lost a lot of blood, but you'll be fine." She stood up and shook her head. "I'm going to head out, before I break an ancient vow of nonviolence by beating your head in. It's your stupid Vida pride that led to all this."

She stormed out. Zachary ignored the healer's brief tirade as he had many times in the past, rubbed his neck and reached to take a large gulp of orange juice. He could afford to lose more blood than most humans, since his body, especially his heart, was strong enough to keep his systems going on very limited resources, but this had been a close call despite that.

He had been sure that this would be the last fight.

He looked up at Michael, who was stretched out with his eyes closed on the love seat, his feet up on the arm, his skin as pale as Zachary's.

"Where's Jay?" Zachary asked. When he had last seen the Marinitch, Sarah had just flung Jay across the room and into the wall.

"Here."

It took far too much effort to turn his head, but when he did, he found Jay sitting on an end table. His arm was in a cast, but otherwise he looked better than Zachary or Michael.

The door burst open, and Zachary cringed, expecting Dominique. Instead, the eyes that swept the room, obviously taking in every detail of the wreckage and injuries, were Adia's. Her voice was barely audible as she asked, "What happened?"

"Idiocy happened," Jay answered. "I didn't . . . up until the very end, I really didn't think she would hurt us."

"Don't call it the very end," Michael grumbled. "We're not dead. But I second the notion of us being idiots. We should have been watching our backs. Zachary's the only one who actually believed it was a trap. Jay and I were twiddling our thumbs like kids at a family reunion."

"And the . . . the targets?" Adia asked. She looked pale, probably disgusted that they hadn't yet reported any success in the face of such blatant mistakes.

Zachary tried to shake his head and push himself to his feet. He felt the world rush into silence; his lips tingled, cold, and black encroached on his vision. He stumbled, ending up back on the couch abruptly. Adia called his name and grabbed his arm to steady him.

"Lay back," she said. "Put your feet up. How much blood did you lose?"

"A lot," he snapped. Mentally chastising himself for the harsh response, he added, "Not enough to be in immediate danger." With a sigh, he added, "I knew it had to be a trap, but I really *wanted* her to be here honestly. When I first sensed her, I thought maybe, just maybe, she was still Sarah enough to fall on the knife instead of inflicting another of those creatures on this world. It's what made me hesitate. I had a perfect moment for a kill, but I thought I saw my cousin in her face."

"Lay down, Zachary," Michael said. "We all feel the same way, but if the brave Zachary Vida is admitting to weakness, we're all screwed."

The brave Zachary Vida. He worked hard to mimic the kind of hunter he wanted to be, and to present an image that was ruthlessly controlled, but it had all fallen apart recently. Had they not *seen* the way he had let the bloodbond get under his skin, or the way he had hesitated with Sarah—or worst, the way he had given up when he felt her fangs at his throat, and let her nearly kill him?

He had told himself and told himself what he knew was true: *It's not Sarah. It's just a monster.* But in the split second when he should have pushed the knife forward, something in him had decided to die instead.

"How many of them were there?" Adia asked. She had always been able to find reason in chaos, a trait that Zachary admired and tried with little success to emulate. He was a good fighter, but Adia could see patterns and come to conclusions faster than the rest of them, and kept her head no matter what the crisis.

"Three vampires," Jay answered. "Nikolas, Kristopher and Sarah. One of the twins showed up first. It looked like Michael had it under control, so I went to help Zachary." He looked at Michael as if for confirmation.

"I figured it was Sarah's boyfriend," Michael said, disdain heavy in his voice. "I didn't even sense the second one until he was practically on top of me. There's something weird about their auras. They get mixed up, so it's hard to tell there are two of them."

"Wait, then who . . ." She looked at Jay's and Zachary's injuries.

"Sarah," Zachary said flatly. "I gave her an opening, and she took it."

Jay nodded, indicating that the same had happened to him. Zachary had barely noticed when Jay had tried to join his fight with Sarah. She hadn't even glanced away but had reached out and flung the Marinitch across the room. Zachary had heard him hit a wall but hadn't seen more of him after that.

Adia crossed her arms but failed to suppress a visible shiver at the notion of Sarah's being the one to inflict such damage.

"It isn't much consolation," Michael said, "but I think I may have taken down one of the twins. I have no idea which I managed to get a knife in, but getting rid of either one will make it exponentially easier to deal with the other. They fight as a team."

"That's something, at least."

It was something they could tell Dominique so maybe she wouldn't decide the three of them were a complete waste of space.

"Hey, what's this?" Michael got up off the love seat to pick up something from the floor. The movement apparently was too much for him, though. He dropped his head as if dizzy and then rolled over onto his back and lay on the floor while he offered the item to Adia. "One of them must have dropped it."

Adia looked at the item, which Zachary thought might be a photograph, and then held it at arm's length before tossing it onto the end table next to him. "That's *sick*," she said.

Morbid curiosity forced Zachary to pick up the picture. The quality of the shot was bad, and the photograph had been scuffed, so it took a minute for his mind to make sense of the swatches of dark and light.

The stream of bright golden color turned into long blond hair. Dark shapes resolved themselves into two figures holding a blond woman gently as they both fed at her throat. Zachary couldn't make out the details of anyone's features.

"Sarah?" Jay asked, peering over the couch to see what Zachary held.

He shook his head numbly. "The picture's too old for it to be Sarah," he said. "But it could still be Nikolas and Kristopher. I guess they have a penchant for blondes."

He dropped his head again and shut his eyes. Jay took the picture from his hand.

"It's not a very useful shot, but should it go in the book anyway?" Jay asked, referring to the immense collection of notes and images that hunters had put together through the centuries to help them identify their prey.

They hadn't decided before the door opened again, this time admitting the one person none of them wanted to face yet.

Dominique froze in the doorway, her cold gaze going from one hunter to the next. Disapproval was clear on her face. Zachary tried to sit up, but the dizziness warned him that standing to greet her would be a bad idea.

"I've already heard reports," Adia said, preempting Dominique's response. "It was a rough fight, but we sustained no losses, and it looks like we have eliminated one of our targets. Also, I have identified a potential contact, so we have a plan for our next move."

Adia was the consummate liar, Zachary knew. He didn't think he had ever seen her turn her ability to manipulate people, situations and information against her own mother, but maybe he just hadn't ever noticed. She wouldn't have made up the possibility of a contact *entirely*, but he wondered if she would stretch the truth a bit to make their successes look more impressive that day. Given that possibility, he knew that right then was not a good time to ask who the contact was or how useful he or she might be.

"And that?" Dominique asked, nodding at the photograph that Jay was still holding.

"One of the vampires dropped it," Jay answered, handing it over.

Dominique's reaction was like Adia's, instant revulsion visible despite her normal reserve. Zachary, disturbed, had to avert his gaze. It wasn't that he didn't know perfectly well why any Vida would be disgusted by the bloodbonds and syco-phants who willingly bared their throats to the vampires. He just couldn't stand to see such a reaction from Dominique.

He rubbed at his own throat, remembering. Sarah hadn't just fed from him. She had gripped his mind and sent him deep into the bliss that Heather had recently described. If Dominique had known any of the thoughts that had passed through his mind as the blood had flowed out, that disgust on her face would surely have been directed at him.

He wanted to hate Sarah for what she had done to him, but he kept recalling the memories she had dragged from both of their minds.

I don't know if I can kill her, he thought as Dominique said, "Foul." She ripped the photograph in half. "Probably left intentionally to make us think of Sarah. This isn't how I want my daughter remembered."

She methodically tore the photo apart. It was the most sentimental thing Zachary had ever seen her do.

He realized he was rubbing his neck again, and shuddered. Dominique glanced at him, her expression back to the calm disapproval he was used to from her, but she didn't say anything. Under the circumstances, his shiver could have been caused by low blood pressure.

"What's next?" Dominique asked Adia.

"Next . . ." Adia paused, thinking on her feet. "Zachary, Michael and Jay will all need some recovery time. I made a contact at that bookstore that may be able to lead us to our remaining targets, but first we need to relocate. If our targets are going to be launching full-scale attacks on us, we should be somewhere less well known and better fortified, at least until we're back to our peak strength. I assume we have a safe house that Sarah doesn't know about." Dominique nodded. Adia pondered a moment longer, then shook her head, declining to continue with her plans. "I think that needs to be our first move. Once we're there, we can recover our strength. Everyone gather only what you need. I don't want to stay in this house any longer than necessary."

Dominique didn't look happy with the delay, and Zachary took the blame for that upon himself, but she didn't argue with the daughter she had put in charge of this mission. Fortunately, though Zachary had been planning to stay with Dominique as long as necessary, he had not yet unpacked his bags. It would be easy to go somewhere else. One house, one bed, one table, was like any other.

CHAPTER 11

"ADIANNA, YOU—" Dominique broke off when her oldest daughter turned to her with a focused expression.

"Yes?" she asked when Dominique paused, reminding herself that she had put Adianna in charge for a reason. Her daughters were—had been—adults, ready for authority, but she had kept them strictly under her command for too long. The recent disaster had made her realize that it was time to make adult responsibilities a little clearer.

She did believe that Adianna was capable, but defying old habits was still difficult.

"I can gather the books," she said, changing her tone from commanding to offering. Even though they did not need the records to identify their current targets, leaving the heavy tomes behind was not an option.

Adianna nodded. "Yes, thank you."

There were two books. One was an ancient tome of Vida law. Every witch of their line was required to study those pages, and needed to be able to recite each law word for word before she was given her primary weapon and named a full member. The second was a collection of notes and drawings about every vampire hunters had ever encountered, currently gathered in a giant binder.

Those invaluable records, representing centuries of knowledge, had been in horrendous shape when Dominique had first seen them, with information, sometimes in other languages, jotted down on scraps of paper, parchment and even bark, often worn, faded or crumbling beyond all readability.

She had sealed the salvageable drawings in archive-quality sleeves, laboriously worked with language experts to translate pieces no one had read in decades, and agonized over her first typewriter in an effort to transcribe and organize what could be read of the older, handwritten notes.

After Jacqueline's death, locking herself away with the occasionally ancient, dusty texts had been soothing. Pregnant with her second child, she hadn't been able to hunt. Sitting, doing nothing—indeed, being *protected* by an eight-year-old orphan child and the human she had married—had been infuriating. She had wanted nothing more than to call up old friends, whose companionship had always been comforting, if not entirely healthy.

She slid the drawing of the twin vampires into the proper

acid-free sleeve and then gathered the books into a canvas bag.

Maybe she *should* have spent those months hunting instead. An unfortunate accident eighteen years earlier might have saved her daughter and nephew from learning what it meant to put a knife in someone they loved.

Please, Dommy.

She could almost hear his voice pleading with her.

Please. You owe me this.

She tried to chase the phantom away. He was long dead. She knew, because she was the one who had killed him. He hadn't been strong enough to do it himself—just as Sarah wasn't strong enough now.

"Did you manage to reach any of our other contacts?" Adianna asked, returning to the room with a duffel bag thrown over her shoulder.

Dominique shook her head, recalling with frustration how her many phone calls had gone. At first she had been able to reach most of the hunters she dialed. They were grumpy and groggy, often having just gone to bed, but they answered.

Some of them told her they would contact her if they got word, but made it clear they had no interest in joining the hunt. Others told her flat out to go to hell. Word must have traveled fast, because after the first round of attempts, she hadn't reached anything but voice mail. The one contact who had asked to set up a meeting had then left a message saying he had changed his mind.

Traitors. They claimed moral objections, but the truth was they didn't want to risk their hides hunting powerful prey, especially when it already knew all their names and faces.

"Our allies know what is going on, but I do not believe any of them will prove useful."

Adianna shrugged, seeming unconcerned. "Might as well keep it in the family."

She looked up into Dominique's eyes as she said it. Her gaze held many questions and a silent plea of *Don't make me do this.*

Adianna prided herself on her control, with good reason, but she was still Dominique's daughter; she couldn't hide perfectly when she looked into her mother's eyes. But though Dominique saw the plea, Adianna clearly already knew she wouldn't respond. They couldn't afford to be sentimental that day.

Dominique would watch her and make sure she didn't balk, because forward was the only direction that would get them through this. She wouldn't let Adianna become another Jacqueline, whose impulsiveness and doubts had destroyed her, along with most of her family.

"I'm going to see if Zachary and Michael need help," Adianna said, looking away. "They're pretty worn down. You check on Jay."

Adianna turned away without waiting for acknowledgement, a gesture Dominique knew had been learned from her. It didn't leave any space for an argument, had Dominique wanted to make one.

Jay had arrived with a backpack and a small tote bag that held all his weaponry. When Dominique reached him, he had finished packing but was struggling with the zipper because of his broken arm.

She reached down to help without asking, or even looking

directly at the empath. Nevertheless, he responded as his line tended to, with no regard for her obvious signals that she had no desire to engage in conversation.

"It isn't your fault," he said.

"A hunter shouldn't try to be a therapist," she said, zipping the backpack and tossing it at him. He caught it one-handed without a problem.

"I just wanted to—"

"It *isn't* my fault," she interrupted. She knew too well the way Marinitch witches worked when they tried to get inside someone's head. "If anything, it's the fault of those damned fools at SingleEarth. If it weren't for their insistence that we honor their alliances, my daughter never would have been put into a situation where she was forced to endure the company of a leech just because he was pretending to play nice."

The Vida line had laws forbidding relationships with their prey—even friendly ones, much less romantic—for a reason. They could all pretend to be human for a while. They could pretend to be charming, even. She had seen it. Believing that they were, however, was a good way to get someone killed.

"You've never once had doubts?" Jay asked.

She answered him honestly, because that was the only way to deal with an empath. Lies only made them pry further.

"Everyone doubts at some point. If we're lucky, we learn better. If we're not, it gets us or someone else killed. If you want to second-guess this situation, do it in your own head. We need a hunter, not a shrink."

She had checked on him. Now, as she returned to Adianna, Michael and Zachary, who were gathered in the living room, she said, "Jay will be right down. Adianna, let me give you the safe house address. I won't be traveling or staying with you."

She had put Adianna in charge but didn't expect her to question the statement, and was not disappointed. This was Adianna's hunt, and Dominique's presence would only undermine her. More important, this was a crucial lesson for Adianna to learn—one Dominique had already studied once before, and felt no need to review.

She had turned to go before she heard Adianna say, "If you're not coming with us, then you're in charge of keeping an eye on Robert. He's conflicted about the vampires, and he and his sister are both young and naïve. He might try to join her or he might try to rescue her, but either way, he could potentially lead us right to our targets."

Dominique nodded. "I know a pair of local shapeshifters—birds—who wouldn't be much use in a hunt but do good surveillance work." If they weren't being called upon to risk their pinfeathers, they would probably even return her call. "I'll see if they can help."

"Good," Adianna said. "You tail the human. Michael, you and Sarah used to hunt in New York City. That area tends to be popular with Kendra's line. Do you think Sarah might go back, if she's looking for familiar territory to feed in?"

"She might go to feed, or she might go to get help from old contacts," Michael answered. "A couple of the hunters we knew in the city were in it more for sport and money than ethics. Sarah might figure they could be allies."

"*Will* they be?" Jay asked.

Michael shrugged. "I wouldn't trust them at my back in a fight against her, which is why I haven't called them to work with us already. But I can check in. If nothing else, I'm sure I can find someone to confirm whether or not we took down one of the brothers. But I'm going to need some rest and food before I'm fit to go anywhere." He rolled his head and shoulders, obviously stiff from the fight. "I have to admit, I'm still trying to figure out how we're still alive."

"You said you think you took one of the brothers down," Adianna replied. "They may have panicked, then cut their losses and run."

"If so, they didn't panic until after one of them had me down and had taken a pint," Michael grumbled in reply. "Once a vamp has his teeth in your throat, he doesn't tend to let go without good reason."

"They may be playing with us," Zachary suggested. "Catch and release."

"Sarah wouldn't be stupid enough to do that," Michael replied. "She knows the only reason they did so well today was because we were surprised."

"*Sarah,*" Zachary said, the emphasis suggesting a convenient label as opposed to the name of the original individual, "wouldn't have stopped if the two others hadn't pulled her off me."

"Nikolas has been known to play with his prey," Dominique said, refusing to acknowledge Zachary's comment on how his fight with Sarah had ended. He knew she was disturbed by it. He wouldn't let it happen again. "He marked Sarah and let her go once before he lured her out to kill her. He may be doing the same with us, in which case it sounds like you all have the *vampire* to thank for your lives."

The words brought the appropriate looks of shame to Michael's and Zachary's faces.

"What matters most right now is that we *are* alive," Adianna said, "and most of our prey will need to rest for the day, which gives us a chance to do the same, and recover. We're not beaten, people. We have a plan. Now, let's get out of here before Kaleo comes down the chimney like some kind of evil Santa, okay?"

Leaving them with that last grim image, Adianna lifted her bags, pulled her keys from her pocket and led the way out the front door.

Dominique followed, the position unnatural to her. It wasn't that she had never followed anyone else—but the last time she had, her guide had been unwisely chosen. That path had ended with a knife in her hand and the body of a fellow hunter in her arms.

As she watched the next generation file out, Adianna in the lead, she wondered if perhaps, just perhaps, it *was* her fault that her daughters seemed to be treading that same dark road.

CHAPTER 12

NIKOLAS WAS IN a towering rage. It should have frightened Sarah—his fury, after all, had directly led to her death—but she could barely focus on it. He was pacing and kept grabbing her arm and occasionally shaking her and shouting, but it was like that only added colored lights to the kaleidoscope of her thoughts.

She couldn't hold on to any single image long; they all slid into each other—one, then the next. Someone was crying across the room, with quick little breaths that made the air quiver. Then there was Nikolas, who was black and white and red. . . . She giggled, reminded of that stupid joke about the newspaper, and he stared at her, but then his features blurred again.

Her skin was buzzing, and her ears ringing. The world was *too* vivid, all light and sound and sensation.

"You have to *focus* now!" Nikolas's anger was tainted by terror, and seemed to make the world roll. "Sarah, *please!*" he begged. "I know what you're feeling right now. It wasn't just your first feed on live blood, but it was *witch* blood. It's intoxicating. Kristopher and I have both been there before. . . ."

The words disappeared from her attention. He was still talking; she just wasn't hearing. Nikolas's voice had ceased to have meaning and had blended into patterns of rising and falling noise.

He grabbed her shoulder and shook her yet again.

"Sarah!" She managed to focus on him for a moment, only to have him throw her across the room. "Is there anything you can do?" he demanded.

She landed on . . . Oh, goddess. She shrieked, because for an instant, in her state, she was on her father's corpse again. There was blood on her hands. Was it his blood? Then the reality came clear, and it was Kristopher lying still and silent on the ground, a ragged wound from Michael's knife in his chest. It hadn't been a heart blow, and the Arun magic wasn't quite as poisonous as a Vida's, but it was killing him slowly nevertheless.

She had to draw out the magic. She could do that. Her powers didn't work the same now as they used to, but they weren't entirely *gone*. She . . .

She glanced up and found herself staring into wide, frightened eyes. Sarah's heart wasn't beating, but someone else's heart was *racing*, pounding, matched by her ragged breaths and the trembling that rippled across the surface of her skin. Nikolas shouted something, and the girl stood and bolted out of the room. Sarah started to rise to follow.

Nikolas grabbed her by the arm and hit her, the blow hard enough that it might have broken her neck if she had been human. Now it was barely enough to get her attention. He snapped, "I swear, if you let my brother die here—" He broke off and shook his head sharply before saying, apparently to himself, "You're going to hate me for this."

What did he—

She couldn't complete the thought. He grabbed her, and then his fangs were in her throat.

And it *hurt*. The buzzing across her flesh turned to wildfire, and her blood turned to lava. The white noise of the world turned to screaming, and the voice behind the screams was hers, until Nikolas threw her away again.

He staggered under the power he had just stolen from her, but he had more practice. He had ripped apart her giddy drunkenness, and now she existed in a cold reality where all she could see was Kristopher's form.

She put a hand over the wound and tried to reach for her magic. Vampiric power wouldn't help her with this. She needed a witch's power, but her Vida magic had fled deep inside, hiding from the new blood.

"I tried to get him to feed," Nikolas said. "That helped when Elisabeth nearly killed us, as if her blood combated her magic. But he wouldn't. I fed for him, on the witch who had attacked him, but I couldn't even get him to take blood from me."

She nodded. The power was already too deep inside

Kristopher for him to rouse enough to feed. Sarah didn't know if she could find her Vida power in time to pull Michael's power from the wound, but Nikolas was right that such power could be drowned with more of the same—normally by taking blood, but there were other methods.

"Come here," she said. She didn't have to say why or ask permission. As soon as Nikolas was near enough, she put her left hand on his throat. He tensed a fraction but did not draw back, even when she pulled at his power. He clenched his jaw; she knew it hurt, what she was doing, but she also knew that Nikolas would never argue against any measure that might save his brother.

Besides, he had taken her blood; he could hear her concerns in her mind. He knew perfectly well that she didn't know how to control her magic anymore, and that she could easily mangle his power through clumsy fumbling, killing both or all of them.

She used herself like a wire to funnel power from Nikolas into Kristopher. She transferred to Kristopher the power Nikolas had taken from Michael, which would temporarily fool the magic of the knife into thinking this body was not an enemy but a friend. It wouldn't completely heal him, but it would slow the damage, like a shot of epinephrine delaying a fatal allergic reaction.

Only when she had given as much power to Kristopher as she dared did she put both hands on Kristopher's chest, one over the wound and one over his heart. She closed her eyes and struggled to find the blade's magic, which she knew almost as well as her own. She and Michael had grown up together. They had trained together. She had helped him form the link between his power and the centuries-old Arun blade.

Bit by bit, she subdued the poison. Now that Michael's magic was feeding Kristopher instead of killing him, Kristopher's own power was able to help heal the wound.

At last, Sarah turned to Nikolas to say, "He'll live. He'll need to rest, and feed when he wakes, but he'll live."

Nikolas nodded, and then it was like that wasn't enough. He pulled her close and kissed her. Through Kristopher, whose mind was still open to her and tightly linked to his brother's, she could sense the overwhelming wash of emotion: protectiveness, gratitude, relief, maybe even love. It was like a reflection on a stream, not as clear as the thoughts she could normally hear from Kristopher, but a background hum Nikolas wasn't trying to hide from her. She didn't want to shut it out, because in that instant she was feeling exactly the same way. Whatever she felt about Kristopher, she did not want him to die for her.

And whatever she felt for Kristopher, she probably shouldn't be kissing his brother.

"Thank you," Nikolas said when she pulled back. There was no sense of guilt in his mind about the kiss. Did he know something she didn't know about Kristopher's feelings for her? Or did he just know that Kristopher wouldn't mind, regardless of his relationship with Sarah?

She had to block out the echoes of thought. It was too much to think about and try to dissect these relationships in the middle of everything else.

"It was my fault Kristopher was hurt," she said.

"It was our choice to come for you," he replied. "We argued over whether or not you had the right to end your own life. We decided it didn't matter if you did have the right. We weren't going to let you go through with it."

Argued. These brothers did not argue, not with each other. Their paths had diverged only once, when Kristopher had chosen to stay with his sister to help her through a difficult time. Otherwise they were always so similar. Sarah's impression had been that Nikolas tended to defer to his brother.

"Out of curiosity," she asked, "what side of the argument were you on?"

Nikolas hesitated. Maybe he thought she might think less of him for believing that they shouldn't ride to her rescue.

"I argued that it was selfish and cowardly to turn yourself over to the hunters," he said softly. "You are a protector. You are not a Vida anymore, but you are still a guardian to those who need you. Your despair is not sufficient to erase that responsibility."

"That wasn't why I did it," she responded. "I would never abandon a duty just because it was *hard*. I didn't want other people—"

"I've seen many people die in the last century and a half," Nikolas interrupted. "The one thing I know for certain is that after you are gone, you lose any power to decide what *other* people do. Will they kill for you? Will they die for you? Will they fight to avenge you? That is never your choice."

It was the people who might kill or die for her if she *lived* who worried her. "What about the humans who come to you and Kristopher to die?" she asked. "Do they get the same talk about whether they have the right to end their lives?"

"They come to us because they see no other choice," Nikolas replied. "When we can, we give them options. I have counseled plenty who come to me seeking an end, sent many home, and given others new lives. Some I can only help one way." He shook his head with a sigh. "Do me a favor, Sarah. If you must end your life, at least do it yourself. Do not force your once kin to slay you, and do not force my brother and me to decide if we must take on the entire race of witches to avenge you. And do it somewhere that I will find your body, instead of my brother. I cleaned up my father's bloody corpse so Kristopher would not see. I can do the same for you."

Only from Nikolas could those words sound sincere, instead of like a ploy to elicit guilt and submission. Sarah knew he meant every word.

At last, what he had said earlier sank in. Kristopher and Nikolas had come to save her, despite knowing she had chosen her death. Would they have avenged her even though she had been willing to give up her life? Would they have either slaughtered or been slaughtered by those she had once called family?

Worse, Nikolas and Kristopher had allies—not just Nissa, but powerful figures like Kaleo. Even if the twins respected her decision, Kaleo had made it clear that Sarah had his protection, yet he was far less likely to care what choice she had made. Would he have joined the fight?

How many bodies would have joined hers on the floor?

She had thought she was doing the right thing. Was Nikolas

correct that she had just been doing the easy thing? As he had pointed out, once she was dead, she didn't have to make the hard decisions anymore.

"What was Kristopher's opinion?" she asked softly. Nikolas had made it clear that his decisions after her death would not be affected by how she chose to die. Kristopher claimed to love her. What would he have done?

"He argued that we are not your keepers, and that no matter how much we want to hold on to you, whether or not you continue with this life has to be your decision." Nikolas shook his head. "Ultimately, it *is* your choice to make, no matter which side of that argument each of us is on. If Jerome had not told us what you were doing, we would not have known. There will be plenty of other moments we will not know about. We will protect you, even from yourself, when we can, but the final decision to live must be yours."

The words cut deeply. She had grown up among absolutes and duty, but Kristopher had introduced her to doubt, and decisions, and therefore freedom. He represented the opposite of all she had been raised to obey without question, so it should not have surprised her that he had been the one to argue for her right to make a decision that now horrified her.

Nikolas, on the other hand, had always been more black and white.

"And if, someday when you aren't there, I decide not to live?" she asked.

Nikolas shrugged, his gaze going distant. "Kristopher will forgive you," he said. "He will mourn for you. He may choose to avenge you even if your death is by your own plan, and I will follow whichever path he takes. But unlike my brother, I do not forgive easily."

Perhaps Nikolas's approval should not have meant so much to Sarah, but the words ate at her, feeding the shame she already felt for—

Oh, no.

"Zachary," she said as the last moments of the fight came back to her. "I—"

"He'll be fine," Nikolas said swiftly, in a flat tone absent all judgment. "You didn't kill anyone; *we* didn't kill anyone."

"Sarah?"

Kristopher's groggy voice shocked her from her thoughts.

She reached for him and helped him sit up. She could tell the exact moment when disorientation broke in favor of memory, because his fear spiked.

"We couldn't let you do it," he said.

"I know," she answered, her voice breathy through her tight throat.

She tried to help Kristopher stand, and then stumbled as a wave of dizziness nearly took her legs out from under her. Nikolas tried to catch them both, and all three of them ended up back on the floor.

"You two both need sleep," Nikolas suggested. "Sarah, I know you slept a couple of hours earlier, but it's well after dawn now, and healing took a lot of energy."

Nikolas insisted on helping them up the stairs; Sarah was so tired she couldn't even focus her thoughts enough to transport herself, and Kristopher couldn't seem to take a step without stumbling over air. Christine looped an arm around Sarah's waist and helped her stay standing long enough to wash her cousin's blood from her skin before she fell into bed. Sarah vaguely recalled her having been in the room earlier, before Nikolas sent her away so she would not be a distraction.

"You should rest, too," Sarah said to Nikolas when it became obvious that he was walking them to their rooms but was not planning on sleeping himself.

"I'll hunt first," he answered, reminding Sarah that while she and Kristopher had been injured, he was the one who had been drained of power. Remembering how much of Nikolas's energy she had siphoned off to heal Kristopher, Sarah was surprised he was still rational. Was his self-control really so much better than hers?

She would have killed Zachary.

He had looked at her, and seen her as Sarah, and called her cousin. Zachary Vida, who never hesitated, had paused, unable to drive his blade into her heart. And in return, she had nearly torn his throat out. If she had had any hope that he might trust her before, how could he possibly forgive her now? She could live, but after what had happened, how could she ever convince any of her once kin that she was anything but the monster they assumed her to be?

Their problems were insurmountable. The Rights of Kin would have them hunted as long as witches lived. Their normal lives could not resume as long as the Vida line drew breath, but Sarah would not let her new allies destroy her mother, sister, cousins and other kin.

She didn't know what to do.

The first step of living this life, though, was learning how to survive. She had tried to ignore her new blood instead of facing it. If she had listened to Nikolas and Kristopher and—much as she hated to admit it—Kaleo in the first place, maybe she could have ended the earlier fight by running, instead of creating the disaster she had.

She needed to learn how to hunt without killing. There were vampires at SingleEarth who never killed, and Kristopher had gone fifty years without taking a life . . . though Nikolas had once strongly implied that the self-control she had seen in him came only at the cost of human life, and that he did not know how to live without death.

She shuddered and tried to shove that thought from her mind. Such doubts would help nothing.

For now, the power she had taken from her cousin and then from Nikolas was sustaining her, but there would be other nights. She needed to know how to *be*. She had never before had choices about who she was and how she wanted to live. All of her life had been dedicated to her duty as a Vida.

As she closed her eyes to sleep, she wondered: was there anything more to her now?

CHAPTER 13

ADIA HADN'T HAD a lot of trouble packing to move to the safe house. After all, she didn't have a piece of sentimental memorabilia that didn't in some way involve Sarah.

She tried to sleep after they settled in, but managed less than an hour before she succumbed to the compulsive need to look up her latest contact. Sleeping would mean letting herself be still, which would mean *thinking*. While she was working and focused on the next steps, she could avoid thinking about the big picture and the overall goal. The oversized binder took up most of the kitchen counter as Adia leaned over it, balanced on a stool.

She had already decided that once she was in charge, all the information was going to be entered into a database, searchable by known characteristics.

Such a system would have made it much easier to find Jerome. Searching by name wasn't effective, since even if he had given his real name at the coffee shop, the book wasn't arranged in alphabetical order. Many vampires weren't known by name, or else were known by several names, so they were arranged by lineage instead. That was why they needed a searchable database.

Dominique had objected on the premise that technology was unreliable and easier to interfere with, but Adia suspected that it was more because Dominique hadn't grown up with computers and didn't trust new things. She was more technophobic than the eighty-year-old woman Adia occasionally handed change to in the subway station.

At last, Adia found Jerome. She smirked at the well-lit color photograph that went with the entry. Though the book held many sketches, there were few photos, because most vampires were smart enough not to get themselves caught on film. This one, however, had smiled for the camera. Stretched out in casual jeans and a T-shirt, with one arm draped over the back of a leather couch the color of good coffee beans, he looked as friendly and welcoming as he had at the Makeshift.

She read the typed entry.

> *Jerome. Kendra's line, changed by Daryl. Rarely outright aggressive, and not known as a frequent killer, but information is diffi-cult to confirm, because he is known for using guile in place of physical assault. No known circuit for hosting, but a frequent guest at circuits owned by a variety of vampires of*

Kendra's and Katama's lines. Jerome does not seem to possess a strong drive toward leadership or power among his own kind but is better described as a game player or information gatherer. He has a wide net of contacts. He seems to court human companions but has no known bloodbonds.

Further down the page, another line had been added in tight, nervous handwriting, as if an afterthought.

Suspected in the death of Frederick Kallison.

There were no more details about that, as if the one line should have been self-explanatory. From the description of Jerome, it sounded like previous hunters had had a chance to observe him pretty closely but had decided he was not dangerous enough to be a worthwhile primary target. If he frequented Kendra's circuit, then hunters had probably encountered him while he was surrounded by much more worthwhile prey.

Then there was that last line.

The name sounded familiar, but she couldn't place it. Frederick Kallison had probably been a hunter, or he would not have been mentioned by name. Perhaps he had disappeared while hunting this vampire, or perhaps it had been known that Jerome had targeted him for some reason. It would be useful to know if Jerome was the type to focus on and stalk particular prey, or if he tended to be dangerous only when cornered. She wondered why the information had been left out.

There wasn't a note about who had recorded this page, though it was old enough to have been included in the mass of entries Dominique had typed when she had reorganized the book. The handwritten note must have been added after that, so someone in Adia's generation probably knew more.

Her nerves were strung so tight she jumped when Jay appeared in the doorway to the tiny kitchen.

"Sorry," the Marinitch said, pausing in the doorway, probably because there was little space to come further forward. "Do you have a minute?"

Their safe house was actually an apartment beneath a gourmet food and wine store owned by one of Dominique's associates. Its size would have been luxurious for one person or perfectly comfortable for two, but it was a little cramped with the four of them—her, Zachary, Michael and Jay—living there. She was indescribably glad Dominique had decided to stay elsewhere.

"What can I do for you, Jay?" Adia asked.

"I fear I may be more of a hindrance than a help in this fight," Jay commented. Adia had a moment to think cynically, *Just like a Marinitch, reliable as a sparrow,* before Jay frowned and said, "You are in charge of this hunt, and I will abide by your decisions. But I think my skills may be put to better use elsewhere."

Adia tried to force herself to think rationally. Jay wasn't the only one second-guessing himself lately, and he didn't have the advantage of rigorous Vida training to help him focus past such doubts. "Your input when we had Heather helped us discover the vampire I am in the process of identifying. I think he will prove to be a valuable lead. If your concern is that your fighting skills are not as keen as your other magic, then—"

"That is not my worry," he interrupted. "I can hold my own. However, I know Dominique and Zachary are better than I am. I feel my presence is weakening *them*. Zachary spends far too much of his attention trying to keep his mind blocked from me, and Dominique has consciously avoided me since she realized my talents. I have been focusing my magic on healing my arm, and it should be fine in another few hours. After that, I would suggest that you assign me elsewhere, so I will not be a distraction to two of our best fighters."

Adia had tried to avoid the issue Jay had just bought to the forefront. She rolled her shoulders, trying to release some of the tension in her neck, before saying, "Maybe you do unsettle Zachary and Dominique. You unsettle *me*. But none of us is going to let something like that get in the way when it comes to a fight.

"Dominique is trying to give us more independence while she does other work. She is still the matriarch of our line and has obligations beyond the Rights of Kin. If she thought she needed to be here, she *would* be. And Zachary *is* here. No matter what he does to keep you out of his head, in a fight he'll be glad to have you at his back."

Jay nodded, though slowly. "You know them both better than I do, so you're probably right. But I thought I could avoid the problem and still be useful by accompanying Michael to New York. I might be able to pick up on information his contacts would not intentionally share."

Adia considered the suggestion. Jay's talents made him

especially useful for information gathering, and given the kinds of contacts Michael had implied he would talk to, she wouldn't mind having another witch watching over his shoulder—especially one with the ability to tell a truth from a lie or glean information Michael's contacts might not intend to share. She would discuss it with Michael when he returned.

Apparently content that he had said all he needed to on the subject, Jay gestured toward the book Adia still had open. "Is that the vampire you found?"

"Yes," Adia answered. "His name is Jerome. The shop seemed to be serving as a kind of mingling place for a bunch of bloodbonds, but it says here he doesn't have any of his own, so I gather he's a bit of a spider. One of Nikolas's bonds, named Matt, came in to speak with him while I was there, so he is definitely linked to our targets." On the off chance Jay would know about something Adia only vaguely recognized, she asked, "Do you happen to know who Frederick Kallison is?"

Jay paused to think, his gaze going distant. "I don't know," he said before twisting to call to the next room, "Zachary?"

Zachary, who had stepped out of the bedroom an instant before, frowned at Jay before crossing the small living room and asking, "Yes?"

Adia posed the question. "Do you recognize the name Frederick Kallison? It sounds familiar, but I can't place it."

It was interesting to watch the play of emotions across Jay's face while Zachary's remained externally calm. Jay turned his head to look at Adia, keeping his face hidden from Zachary, but his expression was pained as Zachary said, "It should sound familiar." Zachary's voice was soft. Adia would not have been aware of how strong a reaction he had had to the name if not for Jay's expression. "Frederick Kallison was involved with a Vida before he died. With Dominique. He disappeared. I was only five, so I don't remember it very well, but she . . ." He shook his head. "Dominique and Jacqueline used to be very close, more like Dominique was an older sister instead of an aunt. After Frederick died, the two of them couldn't talk except to fight. Jacqueline would scream and yell and Dominique would just get quiet and tell her she was being reckless and needed to start settling down. Dominique stopped coming over eventually, and let her father set her up with a hunter he thought was acceptable—your father—like she didn't even care anymore who she was with once Frederick was gone. Jacqueline started going out and staying out for days or weeks until . . . well, until someone carried her body home."

He spoke calmly, almost as if the people he described were distant, unimportant figures to him. Adia watched with morbid fascination the contrast between Zachary's poise and Jay's struggle not to let Zachary see how useless that poise was. He might claim he barely remembered it, but if Jay's reaction was any indication, Zachary not only remembered it, but recalled it with the fear only a child was truly capable of.

It was as if in the past day, she had seen layers to Zachary that she hadn't even known existed. Somewhere inside, he was in fact as vulnerable as a real person.

No wonder having an empath in the house made him so nervous.

"How did that name come up, anyway?" Zachary asked, almost too casually.

Hoping the subject of a target to hunt would be more settling for him, Adia said, "I was looking up my contact from that bookstore, a vamp named Jerome."

Zachary nodded tightly. "I've heard of him," he said. "My impression is that everyone knows him but very few people *like* him, and he pretends to have more influence than he does. I doubt he'll be helpful. And—" He hesitated, and his controlled expression cracked, showing for an instant the fear beneath. "And I'm not sure he's worth mentioning to Dominique," he said. "She's already dealing with losing Sarah. Do you really want to flash in front of her the creature who killed her first love?"

Zachary's reaction was so unnerving Adia didn't know how to respond. The fact was Jerome was the *only* contact they still had, and Zachary and Dominique were just going to have to deal with it. On the other hand, the concept of *her* having to tell *Zachary* and *Dominique* to suck it up was terrifying. These people were the ones Adia looked to for strength, especially now. They weren't allowed to be shaken by a page in a book.

Zachary jumped visibly when the door opened, admitting Michael, whose arms were laden with a bag full of groceries.

"I brought food," Michael said when neither Vida spoke for a moment. "There's one more bag in the car if someone can grab it. Zachary, good to see you up, even if I'm not sure you should be. You're still pale as a sheet."

Either Michael was oblivious to the emotion lingering in the room, or he chose to ignore it. Either way, Adia appreciated the interruption.

She decided she wouldn't mention Jerome to Dominique—or

to Zachary again—if she could find a way around doing so, but she couldn't ignore the only useful contact she had.

Zachary was fraying; he kept lying down and getting up within minutes, as if he couldn't stop his body long enough to sleep. Michael hid behind a cavalier joviality that was driving her crazy, but when he had to be still, he seemed dazed and unfocused.

This hunt was going to destroy them all if it wasn't over soon. Adia just hoped that ending it the way they needed to wouldn't be as bad.

Chapter 14

ZACHARY TRIED TO help put away groceries, until Adia flat out ordered him to leave and get some sleep. As he retreated to bed, he could hear Adia and Michael arguing behind him about how Michael didn't need Jay to "babysit" him when he went to New York. For someone who admitted to working with moral-less mercenaries, the Arun put up a lot of fuss when he thought someone didn't trust him, but it sounded like he might win the argument this time.

Zachary wasn't feeling dizzy anymore, but it was still a relief to stretch out in bed, alone and, for the moment, unguarded. Technically, he shared the room with Jay, but the Marinitch had commented that he had trouble sleeping inside, so Zachary hoped he could get a few hours of sleep without being bothered.

He lay on top of the sheets and closed his eyes in meditation, trying to relax his body and mind. Hearing Adia say Jerome's name, he had wanted to throw up.

He looked up, glaring before he could help it, as Jay stepped into the room in his usual birdlike manner. Jay ducked around the door and closed it behind him before sitting cross-legged on the floor, facing Zachary. So much for not having a roommate.

"Yes?" Zachary finally prompted him, when it seemed Jay was perfectly happy to stare at him with those hazel-green eyes, never speaking. Like a freaking raven, *nevermore*.

Jay would probably be flattered by the description. His line were the only ones who used familiars in their work, raising animals as more than pets. Zachary didn't know what Jay's particular companion was.

"Something's wrong," Jay observed, tilting his head and studying Zachary in a way that made him nervous enough to sit up and erase any lines of anger or concern or frustration from his face from the force of habit.

"What isn't wrong?" Zachary replied. "Sarah is gone, and we're stumbling around—"

"That is not what I mean, and I think you know it," Jay interrupted. "What is it you're ashamed of, that you think I will find out?"

The list was too long to begin, even if he had had any intention of sharing with the birdbrained witch.

"If I thought it was any of your business, I'd say something aloud," he said flatly.

"I'm pretty sure it *is* my business when it starts making you wonder whether you *want* to win, especially since you're likely to be watching my back," Jay replied.

"How about you get out of my head and focus on the problem at hand?" Zachary snapped, grateful that no one who really mattered was around to hear the sharp response. He was exhausted, physically and mentally and emotionally. He desperately needed to sleep. More importantly, he needed a chance to *relax,* to drop all his guards and pretenses and rest.

He knew it wasn't acceptable to need that. The self-control that took up much of his energy should have been real, not feigned, not something so heavy to carry around.

"The problem at hand . . ." Jay shrugged. "I have replayed the event in my mind a thousand times since everything went bad, and I can come to no other conclusion. Sarah was going to turn herself in. She was as surprised as we were when the others appeared. She didn't come there with the intent to betray you."

"Maybe your abilities are not as sharp as you think they are," Zachary said, much more at ease now that the conversation had turned back to their current mission. Focusing on a hunt had often been what had gotten him through the worst times.

Jay smiled, an expression that was strangely sharp and warm and biting all at once. "My abilities are every bit as advanced as yours are, Zachary Vida. They would have to be before I could even begin to read one of your line. And Sarah had every intention of dying the day she approached us. She is desperate, she is scared, and I will say it if no one else will: I do not think she is, or ever will be, a monster. I think we are hunting innocent prey, and I do not like doing that."

Zachary tensed. "Does that mean you would defy the Rights of Kin?"

"Of course not." From most people, the instant words would have sounded insincere, but every word Jay said seemed to be measured and considered. "My first loyalty is to my kin. If Sarah was willing to sacrifice herself, then that shows she, too, is still loyal to that same idea. If we cannot survive without destroying that which shows us what we could be . . . well . . ." He shrugged. "It is an idea I find distasteful, but survival sometimes requires doing that which you would prefer not to."

Finally, Zachary let himself say the words that had been on the tip of his tongue almost since Jay first walked into Dominique's home and introduced himself.

"You creep me out, Jay."

The Marinitch witch laughed. "I think I'll take that as a compliment," he said. "Who's the woman?"

The question was so unexpected that Zachary exclaimed, *"What?"*

There was only one woman Jay could be asking about.

Jay tilted his head inquisitively. "I am not aware of any ancient Vida law that forbids her line from having relationships. So why do you hide it?"

"I don't—" He broke off, because denials were effectively useless. He didn't recall thinking about her, though he knew she came to mind intermittently, especially when he was this tired. "I don't *hide* it. But I don't discuss my personal life with people like Dominique or Adia, either. That just isn't the relationship we have," he said, settling for honesty, since he knew a lie wasn't likely to get him far. "And frankly, it isn't the relationship you and I have, either, so I would appreciate it if you dropped the subject."

There was no law against a Vida having a relationship. It had in fact been hinted to him, strongly and frequently, that he was twenty-six years old and should get around to choosing a partner so he could pass on the Vida genes, like some kind of prize bull. But the only girl Zachary could possibly bring home—so to speak—was one who was capable of taking down a vampire using her bare hands. Anyone he might describe as comforting was no one Dominique would approve of or even want to know about.

He left before Jay had a chance to make any more comments. Adia had ordered him to sleep, and he would obey, but she hadn't said *where,* and he didn't intend for it to be where the telepath could rake his dreams. He obviously didn't have as much control over his conscious mind as he had thought. The last thing he wanted was to give Jay unfettered access to his dreams and nightmares.

He grabbed his jacket, but paused when he realized that Adia wasn't around anymore.

"She went out to follow up on a lead," Jay said when Zachary hesitated.

"She didn't say anything to me."

Jay shrugged, not needing to respond out loud: *Maybe she assumed you didn't want to know.*

She was going after Jerome. Had he really expected her to do anything else? The realization filled him with a kind of fatalistic resignation. It was out of his hands now.

"I'm going out," he said. He took his keys from their hook

beside the doorway. He let his mind be blank, empty, with nothing for the Marinitch to hear. "I have my cell phone if Adia needs to reach me."

He didn't think he had a destination, until he found himself in front of a familiar apartment. He climbed the gray brick stairs and put out a hand like a man who had been hypnotized. He felt like he didn't knock but rather watched as his knuckles struck the turquoise door of their own volition.

The woman who opened the door greeted him with a soft smile.

"Zimmy," she said as she reached forward and ushered him inside. She pulled her hand back at the last moment with a rueful chuckle and held it up apologetically. "Let me just wash my hands and toss a towel over my project."

Her hands were coated in red-brown clay. Her shirt, arms and face had been spattered with it, as well, from the work she had been throwing on a potter's wheel in the corner of the fairly small kitchen.

She put a damp towel over the work in progress, washed her hands and arms, pulled the clip out of her strawberry blond hair to allow it to fall loose to her shoulders in a riot of waves, and put on a kettle full of water before she asked, "Tea?"

"Please," he replied, feeling his whole body relax in her presence. He no longer needed to focus and struggle to keep his breath from speeding and his heart from pounding.

"Hard day?" she asked.

He nodded.

"You look terrible," she said, "like you've been trying to run a marathon in the rain with the flu."

The words made him laugh, the kind of sound that could find its way from his throat only around her, because she was the only one with whom he could accept how utterly empty and absurd his life was.

"My cousin tried to kill me today," he said. He realized that his voice held an edge of hysteria. "She nearly succeeded. But I guess that's fair, since I was trying to kill her at the time."

"Do you need help with her?" she asked.

He shook his head. He didn't know what kind of help she might offer, and he was pretty sure he didn't want to. Michael wasn't the only one whose friends did not live entirely by Vida code. Zachary maintained his relationship with Olivia by never allowing himself to consider the people she was willing to work with.

The kettle whistled, and Olivia poured two cups of tea. She made his sweet, with just a little cream, the way she knew he liked it, and handed it to him in a mug she had made with her own hands and always kept aside for him. She had "given" it to him as a gift, but kept it in her cupboard because she knew he wouldn't be able to keep it anywhere he lived. A beautiful hand-made piece of pottery sitting alongside the generic bargain-store white mugs would lead to too many awkward questions.

By the time he had taken the first sip, his anxiety was gone, leaving only bone-deep exhaustion behind. Olivia sat behind him, on the back of the couch, so she could massage his shoulders.

"So," she said as he shut his eyes and leaned back against her. "Do you want to talk about this horrid hunt you're on?"

"I can't," he answered. Some of Olivia's contacts could probably connect him to his targets, which meant that according to the Rights of Kin, he *should* be demanding answers from her. But he couldn't stand to do so. And since no one else knew about her, no one would tell him otherwise.

"You put all of SingleEarth in a flurry," she said. "I had three appointments cancel this morning." From someone else, the words might have sounded like an accusation, but from her they were as casual as a remark about the weather.

"Sorry," he said anyway.

"Never apologize to me for doing what you have to do, and being what you have to be," she replied, tilting his head up so he met her dark gaze squarely. She slid down from the back of the couch to lean against his side. "You should get some sleep, darling." She ran a hand up his chest, then hooked one finger under the chain barely visible at his throat, fishing the necklace out so she could see it. The pendant was also Olivia's work; she claimed that it was one of her first experiments with silver.

"I can't go home."

She didn't hesitate. "Stay here. I'll have homemade beef stew ready when you wake. You need to get your blood pressure back up. You're much too pale." Before he could comment on her ability to read him so well, she remarked, "I probably know you better than you know yourself."

"Do you know how I'm going to make it through this hunt?"

She paused and kissed his cheek before saying, "I don't care how. I just hope you *do*."

As she returned to the kitchen, he stretched out on the couch. He tried to watch her start the stew she had promised, but his eyelids began to droop. He knew it was a lie, an illusion, but he *felt* safe, and his body responded accordingly, pulling him down into a deep, peaceful sleep.

CHAPTER 15

AS DUSK FELL, Sarah opened her eyes.

She had been dreaming—or remembering. . . .

There had been a girl, a beautiful lady, with honey blond hair and dove white skin. She stood beside a sable horse, one hand on the leather of the saddle, and one hand out like a queen giving a serf permission to rise.

Then a different image. Nikolas, averting his eyes, turning his face away and asking in a very small voice, "Do you forgive me?"

Sarah shoved herself to her feet. Once again, it took too long for her to remember where she was. *Who* she was. She was Sarah Vida, and she was in Nikolas's house, and those dreams hadn't been her past.

She nearly ran into Kristopher as she stumbled into the hallway. He caught her arm to steady her.

Those were his memories. She had healed him but had not had any energy left to shield her mind before they had fallen asleep in rooms divided only by a single wall.

"How do you feel?" he asked.

She meant to say, *Fine*. She meant to say *anything* except for what she said. "Was Christine really so beautiful?"

She wasn't talking about the bloodbond who lived with them now, but the girl of the same name who the twins had loved when they were younger. Kristopher had pursued her despite the difference in their stations, and in the end she had rejected and publicly humiliated him. Nikolas, in a fury, had struck her and killed her.

They had both been human then. More than a hundred years later, the mere mention of Christine still had the power to affect both brothers strongly; just sharing the dead girl's name had contributed to the modern-day Christine's situation.

Kristopher's eyes widened and she felt him try futilely to shield his thoughts from her. "She . . . you . . ." Though she tried to turn her mind away, Sarah couldn't help feeling his distress. Of all the memories he had, the ones of that girl were the last thing he wanted to share. A century and a half later, his feelings about her were still ambivalent. He had loved her; he hadn't really known her. And in the end it had killed her.

"Yes." The answer came from Nikolas, who approached from the stairwell. He must have felt Sarah wake. Perhaps he even knew what she had dreamed, and had chosen to intervene.

"At least, she seemed to be. It's hard to know what she would have looked like through different eyes."

"Do you regret what happened?"

This time, Nikolas looked horrified. "Christine Brunswick was used to having everything she wanted, and she was thrilled to have two desperately infatuated young men tripping over themselves to impress her and answer her every whim. She loved to tease, in private, even though in public she put on her high airs and was too good to even look at us. She was a co-quette. She was a spoiled brat. But she didn't deserve to die."

"I'm sorry," Sarah said. "I shouldn't even have brought her up. I'm not used to dreaming someone else's memories."

"At least the smile is nice to see," Kristopher observed with a forced light tone as he tried to shift the conversation. "What's it for?"

Sarah had been trying to suppress the expression, which didn't seem appropriate for the conversation, but since Kristopher had noticed it, she had obviously failed. She admitted, "I forget sometimes that you two were born more than a century ago. And then I hear Nikolas use the word 'coquette.'"

A cry from downstairs made Sarah spin about, tensing for a fight before her mind recognized the noise as a happy sound.

"Our Christine has a guest," Nikolas said with a wry smile Sarah didn't understand until the three of them reached the living room, where Christine was laughing over a photo album with Heather.

Heather's smile and laughter instantly disappeared as she saw the three vampires. She snapped the album shut, and several loose photos from the back tumbled to the ground. She swiped them up quickly, shoved them back into place and then rose to her feet.

She spoke to Sarah. "Robert asked me to bring some of Christine's belongings to her, after you sent me off with him. That's why I'm here."

Only after the bloodbond delivered the rapid defense did Sarah realize she had always thought of Heather as an extension of Kaleo. Heather must have anticipated that and known that one of Kaleo's agents would not necessarily be welcome in this house.

"I'm glad you're safe," Sarah said. "And thank you for helping Robert and Christine."

Heather visibly relaxed and then let out a sigh. "If you're up, then I'm here later than I meant to be. I should get home." She turned and grasped one of Christine's hands before saying earnestly, "It'll be okay, I promise." She nodded to Sarah, Nikolas and Kristopher and then went through the front door as if she were fleeing.

"What was that about?" Kristopher asked.

"Robert gave her some photos and other sentimental stuff," Christine said, the mention of her brother making her expression warm. "And she brought some of her own pictures, and stayed to talk awhile."

"About what?" Sarah asked, wary. It was nice to see Christine forming attachments to people other than Nikolas, but Sarah wasn't sure how much of a role model Kaleo's favorite, most dependant bloodbond should be.

"About *life*," Christine replied sharply. "About what it's

like to be in this world. I know she's old as heck, but she seems like she could be a friend, and knowing she's been around this long and is happy makes me a little less scared about my future."

Happy, with Kaleo.

Christine's retort to what she must have seen on all their faces was again swift. "Yes, she's *happy*." She started gathering up her own collection of pictures, as well as a handful of camera memory cards. She noticed a photo on the ground and paused before putting it aside.

Sarah glanced at the photo with idle curiosity. Christine didn't seem distressed by the image, but Sarah found it more than a little disturbing.

The photo was old and scuffed and had hardly been high quality in the first place, but enough details were visible for Sarah to get the gist. The woman at the center was kneeling on the floor, one hand tenderly twined in the hair of a man she was kissing. Someone else was kneeling behind the woman; she was leaning trustingly back against him while his lips were locked onto her throat, over her pulse. With them was another woman, who was feeding at the victim's free wrist.

Sarah shuddered. Christine said defensively, "There's nothing wrong with donating blood. I mean, I wouldn't mind, if it were someone I cared about."

The implied offer made Sarah realize for the first time that the hunger was back. She had fed on powerful blood, but then she had spent most of the energy healing herself and Kristopher.

Nikolas saved her from needing to respond to Christine by

reaching between them to pluck the picture from the table. He frowned at it before he told the human girl, "There's nothing wrong with donating, but don't let Heather convince you there aren't any dangers, either. You're safe because you wear my marks, but that doesn't mean all of my kind are always . . . kind." He stared at the photograph, a dark but thoughtful expression on his face.

"Who is she?" Kristopher asked.

"You were with Nissa when Jerome started bringing her to our circuit," Nikolas answered. He glanced at Sarah and then explained, "Jerome is an ally, but not someone I would call a friend. He likes to play with his prey, manipulating their emotions and making them completely dependent on him. Heather can be pretty . . . needy," he said, obviously trying to be gentle for Christine's sake, "but part of that is having been bonded to Kaleo for centuries. This girl was probably one of the worst addicts I have ever seen, and she was still completely human."

"Did you ever—" Sarah broke off, realizing she didn't want to know.

"I never fed on her," Nikolas answered. "And I haven't seen her in decades, so Jerome either tired of her or she gave her throat to the wrong person. Or both." He looked at the photo again and then put it into his pocket. "I'm going to catch up with Heather and return this."

He disappeared.

Nikolas's description had obviously unsettled Christine a bit, but she shrugged at his disappearance and said, "Heather made it pretty clear that we're the lucky ones. Kaleo—" She choked out the word and swallowed before continuing. "She says he treats her well, and protects her. I know not everyone has it so easy." She looked directly at Sarah as she said, "Heather agrees that you'll be one of the good ones. You risked yourself to save her. It made an impression."

Sarah had the sense to control her first response and try to swallow the compliment. It was nice that someone thought she would be a good person even as a vampire, but she wasn't sure Heather's judgment was exactly sound.

"Unfortunately, many of our kind don't make much of an effort to take care of the bonds other than their own," Kristopher said when Sarah struggled to think of a reply. "I have a feeling you'll never be that type. It's something you and Nissa have in common."

The memory that flashed through his mind—and Sarah's—in that moment was of Nissa's horrified reaction the first time she killed. The human she had fed on had abused his hosts' hospitality at a bash in Kaleo's circuit. Specifically, he had insulted Nissa, with Kaleo, Nikolas and Kristopher looking on. He never would have survived the night, but that didn't change Nissa's reaction when she realized she had taken too much.

Kristopher ripped his mind away from the memory—or tried. He couldn't turn away from the memory of Nissa refusing to feed for weeks, or of Nikolas's expression when Kristopher told him he was leaving for a while.

Kristopher stepped back, averting his gaze from Sarah's.

Oblivious to the images running through both of their minds, Christine announced, "I'm going to head to bed. My body can't seem to decide if it wants to be nocturnal or not lately."

They both watched her walk away, and they both wanted to

call her back to act as a buffer between them. There were too many dark thoughts on Kristopher's mind that he couldn't stop and couldn't hide.

If he had just stepped in at that party and stopped Nissa, she never would have punished herself that way. No one in the room had paused to consider how Nissa would react to taking a human life, least of all him. He didn't want to make the same mistake with Sarah. But what would be the mistake? She had been a Vida; she had been a killer most of her life. Who was he to judge?

Is that really how he sees me? Sarah wondered.

Suddenly, Kristopher's thoughts focused, as he made what he felt to be a significant decision.

Enough of this, he thought. *There are better things in this life.*

Sarah's instinctive reaction was unease, and she almost spoke to distract him, before he said, "I have an idea. It's Saturday. In a couple hours, dozens of curtains will be going up in the city." He said "the city" as if Sarah should know which one he meant. "Our people are safe. We've done all we can do for now. So let's go out."

Sarah blinked at him in confusion. What did anything he was saying have to do with *anything* that had occurred so far that morning? "Out . . . where?"

"To a show," Kristopher said. "Maybe a musical—something light, anyway. What would you like to see?"

She almost said, *I have never been to a musical in my life. I have no idea what I would like to see.* Then the absurdity of the suggestion caught her, and without her will she said, "Are you *insane*?"

CHAPTER 16

ADIA RETURNED TO the Makeshift near dusk. The sun set early that time of year, and heavy clouds had rolled in during the day, leaving the world far darker than it should have been at not even five in the evening. The bookstore was still open, bustling with humans who probably didn't have a clue what kinds of creatures inhabited the place after dark. Unfortunately, Jerome was not present.

He might not have been awake yet, but she was impatient. Sitting on the hood of her car, she dialed the number he had given her. If he didn't pick up, she could leave a message asking him if he wanted to get dinner. She was sure he would oblige once he woke.

As the phone rang, she watched a family with three young

children spill out of the closing bookstore. The youngest was waving a book with a blue monster on the cover above his head triumphantly. To Adia, it seemed like a strange sight. She was used to visiting diners and cafés late at night, when her prey was about and there were no children with pom-poms on their knit hats.

When she had been in high school, she had complained about spending time doing "stupid human things" that had nothing to do with her real work. Dominique had given long lectures on discipline and perseverance, while Adia had limped, exhausted, through the school day. There had been no excuses, not for failed fights and not for failed tests.

Never excuses.

She had graduated high school with a grade point average of 3.8.

She had also graduated with a long scar down her back, from her shoulder blade to her hip, gained in a fight in a run-down lot. A vampire had thrown her on top of a mess of junk, then grabbed her arm to pull her up; he had dragged her across a jagged piece of scrap metal.

She had won the fight, eventually. She had bandaged herself, grateful that her kind couldn't get tetanus or hepatitis. And she had never told her mother.

"Hello?"

"What?" For a moment, she forgot who she had been calling. She shook herself, trying to focus. The last twenty-four hours had been too hard, too much. "I mean, hi," she said. "It's Anna."

"Hi, Anna. Everything all right?"

"Yeah," she said, trying to cover for her moment of inexcusable distraction. "It's been a long day, but I was thinking a nice dinner out would be a good way to improve it. Want to join me?"

"I would love to," he replied. "How far are you from Boston?"

"Maybe twenty minutes," she answered. "Are you thinking of somewhere particular?"

He would choose somewhere there would be few witnesses, of course. That would work for her plans, too.

"I'm thinking I'm a pretty good cook, and if you want to go somewhere peaceful and relaxing, I can set a table where we won't have to worry about nosy waiters and other people's screaming children."

You move fast, pretty boy, she thought, while she said, "Sounds lovely."

Jerome gave her directions to what turned out to be a moderate-sized apartment just outside Boston. She doubted it was his only residence; it was probably just the closest address he had to the Makeshift, which he figured would be an acceptable distance for her.

It didn't matter.

A lot of things didn't matter lately. She felt like she was going through the motions, unable to think past the moment to focus on any kind of goal.

She approached the door and knocked, still lost in her own morbid thoughts. She heard Jerome call out, "It's unlocked."

She pushed open the door, and only at that moment did she realize that she had made a grave miscalculation.

Jerome was not alone. Actually, he was more than not alone; he was perched on a stool at a quaint breakfast bar, apparently deep in conversation with an irate-looking vampire Adia recognized as either Nikolas or Kristopher.

Adia had exactly enough time to recognize the twin and note the presence of two other vampires—a man and a woman, curled together on the sofa with an apparently willing victim—before one of the doors in the far wall opened and another familiar figure emerged.

Heather took one look at Adia and began to shriek. The shrill wail was like a siren and was more than enough to startle the feeding vampires so they turned from their prey to Adia.

Four to one, Adia calculated as she took a step backward. There was no space to maneuver in the apartment, she didn't have the element of surprise and—

Five to one, she thought, correcting herself, as someone caught her at the scruff of her neck, propelling her forward into the room. She managed to wrench herself from the newcomer's grip, though she fell awkwardly, hurting her wrist.

Heather's screams had brought her master. It was Kaleo who had blindsided Adia.

"You," Kaleo snarled as the twin started to chuckle in a humorless way.

"Well, Jerome, it's been a ball," Nikolas—Adia was almost certain it was Nikolas—said without taking his eyes from her. "But you look like you're busy here. Have fun."

When Nikolas met her gaze, Adia expected to see triumph, or amusement, or at least relief. He had to know she was hunting him, and now he had a chance to get rid of her without ever dirtying his hands. So why did he just look thoughtful?

No point in puzzling it out now. She had to survive first.

One down, Adia thought as Nikolas disappeared. *Death estimated in . . . maybe two minutes?*

She started to push herself up, only to get kicked in the shoulder by Kaleo. Though not hard enough to break anything, it was hardly a love tap. Pain radiated down her arm.

"Kaleo, back off," Jerome said. "She's my guest."

"Guest. Sure," Kaleo replied. Heather had ducked behind him, and he had one protective hand on her shoulder.

"She is *my* guest," Jerome repeated, "and she is in *my* home. That makes her mine to do with as I will, and that doesn't involve you. Now, perhaps you and Heather should go . . . get a coffee, or something."

And then there were three.

Again Adia started to push herself to her feet, but before she could get far, Jerome knelt beside her. His gaze held an even mixture of solicitous courtesy and warning. She stopped moving.

"Anyone else leaving, or should we just do this now?" she asked, stalling. Her right arm was still tingling; she didn't trust it not to seize up if she went for a knife. She eased to the side, trying to make it look like a painful movement—and it *did* hurt as she put more weight on her right arm to free up her left.

Jerome shook his head, his gaze never leaving hers. The vampires on the couch exchanged glances, and then carried their victim into one of the bedrooms and shut the door.

"I didn't invite you here for a fight," Jerome said.

"Of course not," she grumbled. "You invited me for a romantic dinner, right?"

"Temper, temper, Vida," he said, chastising her. "I think we need to have a conversation, that's all. Now, I'm going to step back and let you stand up. I do not want to fight, but neither will I let you out that door before I have said my piece."

He walked toward the kitchenette, putting a peninsula counter between them. Adia stood quickly, drawing a knife and taking in details of the apartment around her as a matter of course without ever turning her attention from Jerome.

It was easy to tell that he was from Kendra's line. His medium of choice was obviously photography; his work was on the apartment walls, and several photographs had been scattered on the coffee table Adia was standing next to, as if he had been looking for a particular image.

Many of the photographs were of natural features, like glaciers, waterfalls, gigantic waves, slithering rivers of lava and enormous crevices in the earth. Others were candid pictures of people, sometimes sleeping, sometimes with others in friendly or intimate embraces, rarely looking at the camera.

In one, Jerome was dancing with an attractive blond woman. She was in a slinky indigo dress, and her head was tucked down against his chest. The picture wouldn't have been unsettling, except that the one beside it showed the same indigo dress, visible only in brief glimpses around the three vampires feeding on her—Jerome at her throat, and the male and female who had just left the room, one at each wrist. All Adia had to say in favor of the shot was that the vampires had been discreet. They did not hide their own faces, but the photograph seemed specifically angled to conceal the identity of their victim.

Was she dead? Did they hide her face because her lifeless form had showed up a day later, and they knew that this way they could flaunt the crime with immunity? Then again, the main thing she knew about this vampire was that he had no shame or desire to hide his sins. He preferred to flaunt them. She wondered what he told the innocent humans he lured here when they asked about the photographs. Did he feed them some lie, or did he wait to take them here until they were already enough under his control that they wouldn't care?

Jerome had returned to where he had been sitting when she'd first entered, and was just watching her. Waiting for what?

"Can we get this over with so I can get on with my night?" she asked.

He sighed, and nodded as if to himself. Finally, though, he began speaking.

"Can you imagine the terror I felt when I saw Kristopher Ravena lying, near death, with a hunter's blade in his chest?" he asked. As he spoke, he approached her, as if to plead with her for sanity. "When I saw Zachary Vida with his throat nearly torn out by his own kin?"

She circled to put the coffee table between them, and Jerome backed off and leaned against the front door.

"I imagine it was terrible for you—Wait, you were *there*?" She interrupted her wry response as pieces fell into place.

"I hadn't picked up on who you were, but Heather called me a few minutes after you left. I alerted the brothers."

Adia wondered for a moment why Heather had called

Jerome and not Kaleo. Then she realized that it made sense: her intention had been to warn Jerome that the hunters had found his number, and not to protect Sarah.

"You sent Kristopher and Nikolas, and yet you pretend to be concerned that Zachary was hurt?"

"I believed that the brothers would, to the best of their ability, attempt not to harm the hunters, out of respect for their newest fledgling. If I had wanted to ensure the Vidas' slaughter, I would have called Kaleo instead."

"And why didn't you?" Suddenly she was remembering the scene she had returned to, and imagining once again how much worse it could have been. Zachary and Michael had both lost enough blood that they would have been dead had the vampires wished it.

"You believe me now, do you?" Jerome asked.

She shook her head but said, "I'm willing to entertain a conversation about the possibility."

Jerome nodded. "That's about as much as I can expect. In short, the world needs hunters. Immortals need the possibility of their own deaths. And, as I've said before, I am uncomfortable with the concept of wholesale slaughter. But now we have a problem. Dominique has called on the Rights of Kin. So long as that law is in play, it almost guarantees the death of your line, and every other witch line alive."

"A little arrogant, don't you think?" Adia said with a bravado she didn't really feel.

"*Think* about it. If you slay either brother, the other will avenge it. Those two are closer than human twins. They have twined their powers together for more than a century. As a witch, you would be able to see that when you look at them. Neither survives well in separation, and I fear that if one died, the other would simply succumb to madness, and that madness would demand vengeance. And, since both brothers are protected by Kaleo, and Nikolas is one of Kendra's favorites, they would have powerful allies. They would bring most of our line into the fray, and though other lines have tried to rule our kind, Kendra's line has always been the deciding factor. The result would be a war, and your stupid, *stupid* kin would keep fighting it because of a law written by a scared little girl who had just witnessed her mother's murder thousands of years before either of us was born."

Adia had been so wrapped up in his words she was startled when he fell silent and she suddenly realized he was much closer than he should have been. She moved to raise her knife, and he shoved her backward, sending her off balance—but only long enough for him to step back again, keeping her from attacking.

"What option do we have?" she asked. "Should we just forget all the deaths this generation?"

"Do you want to *survive*?" he snapped.

"Sacrificing all we believe in to preserve some semblance of our flesh would destroy our line as surely as any of your kind could." She had already accepted that this might be the end. If their line had to die, she would rather die with dignity than beg for leniency and fade into obscurity.

"I've seen enough genocide in my time, witch," he said. "You don't want to choose that path. Find an option. Be creative. Use some of the wit and intelligence I know your line possesses and come up with *something*." She started to object, but he spoke over her. "And don't give me that line about how Vidas don't compromise or make deals. It's crap. There is no such thing as perfection."

"Maybe not," she admitted, thinking of the many mistakes she had made in the past day alone. "But that doesn't mean we stop trying."

Jerome shook his head. "Would you like to see what perfection looks like in reality, Adia?" he asked.

There was a challenging light in his eyes, along with a hint of anger. Part of her wanted to rise to that challenge, but part of her sensed that if she did so, she would regret it.

Refusing, however, had never been a choice.

CHAPTER 17

SARAH GAPED AT Kristopher, struggling to control her anger and the bloodlust that seemed to rise and tangle with it, like the two were feeding on each other.

Her family was trying to kill her. As if that weren't sufficient, she had dreamed Kristopher's memories of his dead first crush and then heard from Kaleo's favorite bloodbond that she would be a good little vampire, before having a short discussion about how vampires occasionally utterly ruined human lives for fun. Then she had a flashback to Nissa's committing murder, and now Kristopher thought he could fix it all up with a *Broadway musical?*

Kristopher seemed taken aback by her response. "I thought

it would be nice to spend an evening focused on something other than a situation we have no power to change right now." Though he didn't say it out loud, and tried to squash it before she heard it, another thought sneaked through to her: *I want to show you there are still things in the world worth living for.* "If you don't want to see a show, we could do something else, anywhere we want. Have you ever wanted to visit the Louvre? It's past ten o'clock in Paris right now, but I could call Kendra, and she could have it opened for us."

The words felt like a blow. She was on the verge of tears and had *no idea why.*

"Damn it, Kristopher!" Sarah shouted. "You nearly died today. I nearly killed my cousin. We are being made top priority by every hunter my mother has ever met—including everyone I ever called family. Your people are in danger, mostly because you and I showed absolutely no common sense or self-control—"

"You chose to live your own life," Kristopher said challengingly.

"I didn't *choose* anything. You chose for both of us, remember?"

Kristopher had waited, perfectly mellow, through most of the tirade, his expression clearly asking, *So?* It was only then that he flinched. "Then let me do something right this time. Let me show you something beautiful. Do you like—"

"Kristopher, *please,*" she begged before he could finish the question. "I know you're scared for me." His anxiety and guilt were pummeling her, no matter how he tried to suppress them. "I know you think this will make me feel better. But this isn't what I need right now."

He nodded slowly, but she knew he was humoring her more than agreeing. He was so sure that if only he could show her his world, she would be able to accept it as fully as he did.

Nikolas cleared his throat, alerting them both to his presence. Sarah turned, wondering how long he had been standing there and how he would respond. She hadn't needed to read Kristopher's mind to see that she had hurt him. But Nikolas's expression was strangely shuttered, impossible to read.

"Kristopher, I checked in with Nissa while I was out," Nikolas said. "A lot of her people normally rely on Single-Earth, and she's having trouble finding them all safe havens. Her people tend to trust you more than me, so I thought you might be in a better position to help. I'm sure you could do so and still get back in plenty of time to make curtain on Broadway." Had he been standing there long enough to hear the idea, or had he known ahead of time what Kristopher had planned? Or did he just hear Sarah's reeling reaction in her mind?

Kristopher nodded. "Sarah—"

"Go see how your sister is doing," Sarah said. She had barely even thought about Nissa since they had first established that she was safe early that day. She hadn't thought about the strain Nissa's nonviolent friends must have been under. As a peace offering, she added, "What time would the show start?"

Suddenly, Kristopher's smile was bright. "Most shows on Broadway open at eight. I'll pick you up at seven-thirty?"

She was able only to nod. Kristopher looked like he wanted to say more, but he disappeared instead, leaving her staring at where he had been. At last, she turned to Nikolas and said, "Thanks."

"Nissa needs the help." He shrugged, and admitted, "But she probably would have let me provide it."

"He just . . ." Her voice trailed off. She didn't know what she could say to *anyone,* much less to Kristopher's brother.

"Kristopher forgets," Nikolas said, "that it was two years after our deaths before Kendra fairly literally dragged us to our first opera."

The words surprised Sarah, as they cut deftly to the heart of her earlier anger. She had studied Kendra's line, and knew what kind of magnificence most of its members had created even before they were changed. Sarah, who had never set foot in an art museum or been to so much as a high school play or a slam poetry recital, was now surrounded by immortals who had steeped themselves in the arts for years—centuries, even.

"I always assumed you were raised with all this," she admitted to Nikolas.

"We couldn't afford it," he replied bluntly. "When Kaleo was courting Nissa, he would bring us art supplies. He would bring art books and describe some of the wonders of the world. But for some reason," he said, his tone ironic, "Nissa wasn't comfortable with the notion of his taking us into the city or around the world to actually *go* to a museum or a theater."

"I still feel like I can't afford it," Sarah confided. "There is so much to deal with right now, it seems like a bad time to pick up hobbies."

"I would argue," Nikolas said thoughtfully, "that now is an excellent time to discover what beauty the world has to offer, but if you are not ready, then we may as well focus on the task at hand. Survival, right?"

She nodded. "The hunters—"

"Secondary," Nikolas said with the same cool determination she had seen in his eyes when they had fought. He held out his hand to her. "Come with me."

She hesitated. That expression made her nervous. "To where?"

"To deal with the primary problem that makes you a danger to yourself and others," he answered, "so we can lessen some of your fear, and hopefully allow you to relax and see a marvel of voice and body and light and language this evening."

Sarah cautiously reached out to take his hand. When their fingers touched, Nikolas willed them both away.

She found herself a moment later in some kind of club. The music wasn't too loud, but the dim lights and the crowd made everything seem more overwhelming. The sudden, overpowering scent of humanity—their sweat and blood as the people mingled—didn't help. She had to shut her eyes for a moment to block out the tapping of a hundred pulses against her brain.

"Where are we?" she asked once she had stabilized herself against the unanticipated smells and sounds of life around her.

"Phaethon. It's a semi-exclusive Manhattan establishment catering to independent musicians," he replied. "These are normally Kendra's hunting grounds, but she won't mind my bringing you here."

Hunting grounds. She wondered how old the business was; she had never heard of it before, though as a Vida, she had of course made a point to keep track of such places. "You brought me out to hunt?"

"To feed," he replied. "This is the kind of place where it is easy to find a willing donor. They know this establishment is Kendra's, and that members of my line come here, and therefore know to seek us out here. I have trouble imagining your hunting down an innocent on the street, but somehow I suspect you will also have trouble asking those you already know, such as Christine, to bare their throats to you."

Sarah had tensed, looking around her in an entirely new way. "Nikolas, I don't think I'm ready for this."

"I don't think you have a choice," he answered. "Christine told me what happened, though she did not fully understand how much danger she was in. I know that your fear of hurting her is what nearly drove you onto a hunter's knife. It is my responsibility to make sure you are not a danger to my people. Kristopher isn't hard enough to push you into this, but you do not have a choice. You need to learn to feed."

"I won't kill."

There, she said it, and in saying it she acknowledged their major difference: Nikolas, for all his black and white charm and talk about being a protector, was a killer. He had been in jail for murder when Nissa had changed him to save his life, and then Kendra had taken him for his first hunt and taught him to kill as a vampire. He was known in the human world as a serial killer, and long before, he and Kristopher had killed Sarah's ancestor, Elisabeth Vida.

Now he nodded. "I wouldn't have taken you here if I thought you would kill," he said. "You know Kristopher and I will never judge you if you pick up such habits, but you do want to be cautious about it. Before you ever feed, you should be aware of whose territory you are in. You must know that the mortal whose throat you bare is yours to take. Humans in this place are under Kendra's protection."

Sarah nodded warily. "We're still left with me needing to pick up a complete stranger to assault."

Nikolas shook his head. "No, we are left with you needing to be charming long enough to make the acquaintance of one of the many humans in this place who would be honored beyond belief to be chosen."

That's disgusting, she thought. She managed not to say it out loud, but knew that Nikolas could hear her thoughts, so it certainly wasn't his sensibilities she was protecting.

"Better or worse than choosing an innocent, like a lion pulling down a gazelle?"

She glared at him, because his being right didn't make this any easier. "I saw your expression earlier, when you talked about that girl in the photo. Even you thought it was pathetic. What makes these humans any different?"

"These humans," Nikolas said, looking around, "have lives, and passions. Those that choose to bleed have their own reasons, ranging from the feeling of power they get from knowing we need them in order to survive, to the fact that the sensation itself is pleasant. The ones I pity are those who have given up everything else. They bleed because it's the only way they can see to get through the day."

Sarah shuddered. "And what causes that need?"

"If one of our kind takes a human without much to live for and rolls their mind too deeply, they'll fight to keep that feeling," Nikolas answered. "Most of them recover, in time, if they want to, unless someone like Jerome doesn't give them a chance. I'll be right beside you tonight, so you don't need to worry about endangering your donors."

"I wasn't . . ." Okay, she was worried, but only because her experience as a hunter had made her believe that there really was only one kind of bleeder in the world: the pathetic bash-bunny who didn't care if he or she woke up or not. "I believe you that you'll keep them safe, so I'm *trying*. But I don't know how to . . . you know."

Nikolas shook his head, chuckling. "Shall I demonstrate?"

She wanted to say no. She wanted not to be here.

She *wanted* not to be a vampire, but permanent death was the only alternative to her current state, and she had chosen not to take that route.

"Please?" she managed to say softly.

Nikolas was right that she needed to do this, but she still wasn't sure if she *could*. He could show her how to pick a donor or instruct her in whatever technique went into the feeding, but how could he teach her how to forget the last eighteen years?

CHAPTER 18

SARAH WATCHED NIKOLAS sweep the room with his black eyes. He narrated his thinking and his conclusions as he did so.

"There are people here who have no idea what we are, and others who come here specifically to meet us. The first trick is to figure out which is which." His expression as he sized up the individuals in the crowd was serene, not predatory, despite his purpose. "There are a few obvious signs. The girl in the turtleneck sweater is probably not seeking one of us. Same for the Goth boy in the corner with the spiked dog collar. Most mortals who come here seeking each other look around. They examine other people, send flirtatious smiles, buy each other drinks. Some of them come here just for the atmosphere, in which case they are usually either attentive to the music or have brought something that clearly tells other humans they are not here to be picked up."

He nodded to individuals as he spoke, drawing Sarah's attention to the courtship rituals going on around her, as well as the obvious *not interested* signals some individuals were sending out.

Nikolas offered little further instruction. He focused on a young woman who was sitting in a corner booth, sipping a coffee and doodling in a notepad in front of her. Every now and then she looked around her, but she didn't seem to focus on anyone or anything.

When Nikolas first approached, her expression was wary, which was unusual. Nikolas was handsome enough to turn heads in most situations. However, as he moved closer and she got a better look at him, it was as if she relaxed. She smiled a little shyly, and Sarah heard the human's heart begin to beat faster.

Nikolas slid into the booth next to the girl as she moved aside to let him in. He ran fingers through her hair, and without any pressure from him she tilted her head to the side, baring her throat. There had been no words exchanged between them. As Nikolas had said, this girl already knew what she was seeking, and what Nikolas was seeking.

Sarah looked around, concerned. Wasn't anyone else seeing this?

But no one else was looking. No one cared. Sarah had seen it a hundred times at the parties she had crashed; one human bled, and the rest were completely *blind* to it.

As she turned away she found a young man, no more than a year or two older than her, watching her. The instant Sarah looked toward him, he dropped his gaze. Then, when he realized she was still looking at him, he raised his eyes again. He stood but then hesitated, as if not certain whether to approach her.

He was attractive in a clean but scruffy way, with hair that was a little long—not as if it was intentionally styled that way, but as if he hadn't had time for a haircut lately—and skin that would probably have benefited from spending more time in the sun. His eyes were a warm brown, questioning as he looked at her.

He looked like he was someone's son or brother, the kind of person she used to try to save when she went out hunting. She wondered what he did when he wasn't here hoping someone would come to use him. Was he in school? Did he have a job? Did he have dreams, beyond the wish that sometimes an immortal would have him bare his throat and drink?

She couldn't see him as prey, as food. She simply *couldn't*. She knew she needed to feed; she had resolved herself to that truth, and it wasn't that she was refusing now, but she didn't know how to see this obviously willing young man as a source of sustenance instead of as a human being.

She approached him, trying to fake more confidence than she felt. He smiled as she appeared to make up her mind, and then he seemed confused when she sat across from him instead of next to him as Nikolas had done with his chosen prey.

"Hello," he said while she struggled for words. His tone was partially polite, partially friendly and more than a little questioning. He searched her gaze . . . no, her eyes. With her transformation, her Vida-blue eyes had changed to black. He was confirming what she was.

"Hello," she replied. And though she kicked herself for it, she added, "What's your name?"

"Jake," he answered. "Jake Frose. I saw you come in with Nikolas." He left all the associated questions unasked.

She looked at Nikolas, who was just pulling away from the young woman he had chosen—or had she chosen him? It was hard to tell, especially considering that Jake had surely picked Sarah out before she noticed him. Nikolas said a few words to the girl and then flagged down a waitress for her before coming to Sarah's side.

"Jake." He greeted the young man with a smile. "You aren't performing tonight, are you?"

Jake's face immediately took on a glow when Nikolas recognized him and addressed him by name. "Not tonight," he answered.

Nikolas explained for Sarah. "Jake performs here a couple nights a month. He's a student at the Brooklyn College Conservatory of Music and one of the local artists that Kendra sponsors. He has a singing voice that can break your heart."

Jake ducked his head modestly but did not deny the praise.

Nikolas continued with his usual assertive honesty. "Jake, my friend Sarah is very new to our world, and she had a less than glowing impression of what that world is like until recently."

Jake's eyes widened with surprise, and he blurted out, "You're the hunter?" He immediately blushed and said, "I'm sorry. I've heard of you. Most of us have heard of you."

Probably not in flattering ways, Sarah thought, given her recent occupation. Yet he was being nice to her. She didn't understand. Was he that desperate?

He seemed to have grasped her concerns. He said to Sarah, "Kendra made it clear to me when I first met her that I don't owe anything to anyone. She pays a lot of my bills, but she asks for music in return and nothing else. Anything else I give, it's because I choose it, because I want to."

"Why?" Sarah finally managed to ask.

So many of the bleeders she had met didn't care if they lived or died, just as long as they could bleed. They gave up everything else, betrayed other humans to the vampires, sacrificed their dignities and their souls for the feeling that came when there were fangs in their throats.

Was Jake one of those?

Jake shrugged. "Why not?" he asked. "It doesn't hurt, and it doesn't injure me. I don't donate on performance days, but other times, I don't mind. Look . . ." He stood up, hesitated just a moment and then sat by Sarah's side. "I'm offering," he said. "I know you won't hurt me. Nikolas won't let you, even if your self-control isn't perfect yet."

He sat close to her, as if he would kiss her. He reached out to touch her cheek and then closed his eyes, turning his head to the side to bare the long line of his throat.

Nikolas set his hands on Sarah's shoulders and said, too quietly for Jake to hear, "You've had that Vida control clamped down so tightly, you're not even letting yourself acknowledge him with your senses."

I don't want to do *this!* she thought, glaring at Nikolas with a spike of frustration. How long before had she almost ripped out her cousin's throat? Nikolas gave her an even look in return, waiting, trusting she would pull herself together.

She drew a deep breath and focused on Jake. She was trying to steady herself, but instead the inhalation brought to her the scent of his skin and the blood beneath. She had to drop her control inch by painful inch, consciously acknowledging the senses she had learned as a hunter to respond to or ignore as survival made necessary.

As if he sensed the right moment, Jake pulled her forward. The rhythm of his heart and blood and breath made a symphony, and she let herself drown in it.

That was his metaphor, not her own, she realized as her fangs pierced his flesh ever so gently. The embrace was intimate as his thoughts wrapped around hers, sharing what he felt: peace, joy, *music*. His entire world was music, rising and falling in people's voices, in the tremble of lights and colors. He heard music even in silence and was constantly composing it from the sounds of the world. And his greatest art came from this sensation of oneness and sharing and *being* with eternity.

She felt Nikolas's hands on her shoulders squeeze a warning, but she didn't need it. Instincts compelled her to draw back before she went too far, and she knew she would never risk harming this beautiful, perfect instrument.

She let him go, and he leaned back in his chair, dazed but unharmed.

Sarah blinked and realized there were tears in her eyes.

"Now you know why Kendra chose him," Nikolas said.

Sarah nodded. "Thank you," she whispered to the artist before her.

His eyes fluttered open just long enough to focus on her. "Come back and see a show sometime," he said.

"I will," she answered, and she meant it.

Once again, Nikolas waved to one of the passing waitresses. He gestured to Jake, and the woman nodded in return.

"They'll take care of him," Nikolas said. "We should move on."

Sarah nodded again, mutely, and followed as Nikolas led her away. She felt like she was still sorting through the crescendo of thoughts she had encountered. Was this how Kristopher experienced the world? If so, she could understand why he had thought that even with the Rights of Kin hanging over her head, she would want to see a show or visit a museum.

"Don't fight it," Nikolas advised. "When they're willing, and unafraid, they share so much of themselves with us. Let it stay with you awhile."

"When you talked about Kristopher going to live with Nissa, and about your trying to learn to hunt without killing, you acted like it was hard to survive that way," Sarah said, speaking carefully, hoping not to offend him but desperate for the answer. "Even before you pulled me away, I was going to stop. It seemed like it would have been a tragedy to harm him."

"If you feed regularly," Nikolas replied, equally exactingly, "on willing donors who have a firm sense of self, you will rarely be tempted to harm them. Over time, the instinct will arise, and it will take either death or stronger blood to sate your hunger. If you are careful from the start, there are options that do not involve death, but fledglings taught to kill early have fewer choices."

He was standing tensely, but he had not looked away, as if he knew she needed these answers. The encounter with Jake had made her reevaluate everything she had ever thought about the humans who willingly shared their lifeblood with vampires, and everything she had ever thought about the creatures who accepted that gift, but she still needed to know: what would she become, and was it something she could abide?

Nikolas continued, "I believe the shape of the power itself changes from the moment of the first hunt. There are those among us who say fledglings should kill the first time they feed, and that those who do not permanently limit their power. Perhaps it is true. What I have seen in the past century, and heard from others of my kind, is that those who kill in their first nights among us are driven more often to kill in the nights after."

"You didn't think it would be good to tell me this before I fed?" Sarah asked.

Nikolas shrugged, in no way defensive. "Knowing wouldn't have changed your decision, and you would have trusted me less tonight if you suspected I might have had any motive to encourage you to kill. I will answer questions you have, but I have no reason to volunteer information that will do nothing but make you uncomfortable."

"What about Kristopher?" Why hadn't *he* told her this, when he knew how afraid she was of turning into a killer?

"In my brother's defense, these are only thoughts I started

having after he left, when I began to wonder why it was so easy for Nissa to survive without killing, and why Kristopher was able to survive with her, but it seemed impossible for me to do the same. Kristopher probably never had reason to give it any thought."

Sarah nodded slowly. Trying to rally her courage, she said, "I think . . . there may be a few things your brother hasn't had a chance to give much thought."

She remembered his reaction to her sharing his memories of Christine. It hadn't been feelings of love that had washed over him right then, but obligation.

She had seen the way these brothers lived, the bonds they surrounded themselves with and the way women reacted to them in general. She had accepted that Kristopher had probably flirted with hundreds or thousands of pretty girls in his lifetime, without any thought of "forever." The only thing that made her different was that she had ended up dead when he hadn't intended it.

Nikolas looked like he was about to remark on the subject when another voice interrupted them, saying, "Hey there, stranger."

The problem with hunting in Manhattan, Sarah realized suddenly, was that she used to *hunt* in Manhattan . . . or if not on the island, at least near it. Even if it had occured to her earlier, with almost twenty million people in the New York metropolitan area, Sarah would have been comfortable with the likelihood of not running into anyone she knew. Unfortunately, luck had not been working in her favor lately.

Now the familiar voice, with its cautiously friendly tone,

caught her off guard. Habit told her to smile and return the greeting warmly. After all, she and the hunter who hailed her at that moment had always been close.

She turned to face the witch, with no idea what she would do next.

CHAPTER 19

JEROME TURNED AWAY, but even though the vampire's back was to her, Adia felt unable to move. She watched as he retrieved one of many small boxes from a closet on the other side of the room and set it down on the counter.

"Some of my favorite photos can't go on the walls," he said, as if making casual conversation. Given the photos that *were* on the walls, Adia wasn't sure she wanted to contemplate what this vampire would find too objectionable for public display.

He opened the box and flipped through the stack of photographs therein before selecting three, which he presented to her, fanned out so she could see the images even without taking them from his hand.

She stared at his face for a moment, strangely unwilling to

look down at what he was showing her. She had seen enough of the "art" he put on his walls to know he liked to immortalize his victims. Did she really *want* to look?

He stood there patiently for a moment and then put the photographs down on the table. "I hope you'll leave them here when you go. I don't have copies." Then he disappeared, in one irritating blink of an eye.

At last, alone, Adia looked down at the three pictures he had decided to share.

The first one showed the same beautiful blond woman, in her bright indigo club dress, looking up at Jerome as he reached out a hand as if to pull her into a dance. The expression on her face was ambivalent, equal parts uncertainty and daring joy. The lights had caught a sparkle in her bright blue eyes.

Adia had never seen the girl in the photograph, but she recognized her. She knew exactly who she was.

The next image was of the same woman, now in casual clothes, stretched out on a couch, snuggling with Jerome but looking directly at the camera with a distressed, startled expression that was incongruous with the relaxed posture. Adia knew perfectly well why she hadn't wanted her picture taken at that moment.

The last of the three photographs was of a different couple, but the tone and content were similar.

Adia gagged hard, shoving herself away from the table with the photographs as if they had a poisonous bite.

She stumbled out the door and nearly sprinted to her car. She had to . . . had to . . .

Behind the wheel, she nearly fishtailed as she U-turned out

of her parallel parking space. She had to get home. No, not home; she didn't really have a home right then, just the safe house. But she needed to get *there*. She needed to ask . . . needed someone to *explain,* to make things right . . .

How could they?

An hour before, Adia would have said she knew what betrayal felt like, what anger felt like, but she would have been wrong. She had felt nothing compared to this, which made her turn the key and walk into the safe house in a bubble of her own anguish.

Jay, who had been sitting at the kitchen counter, eating, physically recoiled from her. He started to fight that instinct and came toward her as if to comfort her, but her glare stopped him in his tracks.

"Where's Zachary?" she asked. Her voice came out soft. She had almost expected to hear herself shout, but her lungs were too tight.

"Shower," Jay answered as Adia became aware of the sound of running water. "He got home just a minute ago. We were going to go out to—"

"Hush," she snapped. She stormed through the apartment and pounded on the door to the bathroom. "Zachary Vida, you have fifteen seconds to get out here or I swear by my blood I will drag you out."

The water turned off instantly. She heard the rustle of clothing, and the door opened with seconds to spare, Zachary not completely dry, wearing only his pants, a towel over his shoulder and a necklace she had never seen before. Eternity. How ironic.

"What's wrong?" he asked, eyes wide. "What happened?"

For a few seconds, she stared at him, trying to convince herself it wasn't true.

"Adia!" he snapped. "Take a breath. Get a hold of yourself."

She managed to choke out the words: "Did you know they took a picture?"

He shook his head. "I don't know what you're talking about."

"Zachary—"

They both spun on the Marinitch witch when he tried to interject, Zachary silently, and Adia saying, "This is *not* the time, Jay!"

"There never *is* a time!" Jay snarled back.

"Shut up!" Adia had felt like her world had been shattering for days, but now it was as if it was gone. Everything had fallen down, and she was standing in the middle of emptiness, and every guide she had ever known had failed her. "Zachary, how *could* you?"

"What—" He stopped arguing long enough to examine her expression. He didn't protest his ignorance again. Instead, he paled. "I didn't—" He looked toward Jay, who apparently wasn't going anywhere. In another mood, Adia might have cared, but she couldn't stand to put off this confrontation, and at that moment she wasn't experiencing a lot of pity, either. "Adia, do we have to . . ." Finally, he whirled away, his fist impacting the door hard enough to make it shudder. "It isn't like that!" he shouted.

"Why don't you tell us what 'it,' whatever you two are going on about, *was* like?" Jay suggested, the tension in his voice an echo of their own, though he obviously had himself more under control. That was new, the Vidas losing their minds while their kin stayed calm.

Zachary stood next to the couch, his fingers digging into the back as if he needed the support to hold himself up, as he answered in sharp, biting words, "I had a fight go south, a while back. I lost. I lost bad. At the end of it, three of them were pinning me. I was too run down to use power to throw them off. They stripped my weapons. And they offered me a choice. They could turn me over to the others, who would kill me, probably slowly—and that side of the offer was described in *great* detail by some of the vamps who were there watching—or I could agree to let them bleed me a little, and then they would let me go."

He hung his head, making his decision clear.

Vida law forbade making deals with the vampires, even to save one's life, but that law was designed to keep witches from betraying each other or sacrificing their beliefs as part of a deal with a creature who could not be considered trustworthy. Zachary had made a mistake, but it wasn't an unforgivable one, in Adia's eyes.

"That's it?" she asked. She had seen only one photograph of Zachary. It was possible it hadn't been like the other ones, that it really *had* been just one fight gone bad. Jerome could have been messing with her. He would have known she would assume the worst, given the other images.

But Zachary shook his head. "After that, it ate at me. I got sloppy. I think part of me was trying to lose fights, so they would kill me and I wouldn't have to admit to the rest of you . . . or to myself . . ." He dared to look up a minute, but whatever he saw in Adia's face made him look away again.

Jay said, "You lost a fight, Zachary. That's not worth losing yourself over."

"You don't understand," Zachary replied, his tone utterly flat.

Adia shook her head. "Zachary—"

"No," he interrupted. "Just . . . no. You know perfectly well I couldn't tell you. I certainly couldn't tell Dominique. I couldn't tell anyone except—" He swallowed thickly.

Adia saw Jay's eyes widen as if he knew something Adia didn't know and had just made the connection.

"Believe it or not," Zachary said slowly, "vampires will pick out their favorite hunters. And other vampires know about it. My 'patron,' as she puts it, made it clear to me that she wouldn't reveal me to others of her kind, but that if I got in trouble, I could say her name and she or one of her associates would come get me. I swore up and down I'd never use it, and I never have, but she and her friends frequent a lot of the rougher circuits, so sometimes I don't need to. I'll be in a fight, and then suddenly it'll be over and . . ."

When it became clear that he wasn't going to say more, Jay asked, "The guy who helped Nikolas pull Sarah off you was one of your friend's friends?"

"What guy?" Adia asked, startled . . . and yet not. Jerome had said he had warned the twins, and that had been when they had found the first photograph, which she realized now hadn't been left accidentally. It had been a message, though not to her.

"I didn't see him, since I was locked in the closet at the time with a broken arm," Jay answered. "I just heard his voice."

"Jerome," Adia said.

Zachary flinched and nodded. "I'm sorry, Adia."

"Why didn't you ever talk to me?" she asked. "I'm not Dominique, Zachary. You could have told me what was going on, and we could have worked it out. We could have gone after them together, or just—"

"Because you needed to be better than I was!" he shouted. "Adia, I know I'm weak. My entire side of the line is. My mother went mad after my sister's death. She went out, and never came back. My little brother followed her, and we never saw him again. The only reason I've survived is because Dominique looked out for me, and you know what kind of perfection she demands. I couldn't spread my weakness to you and Sarah."

"There is no such thing as perfection, Zachary," Adia said, aware she was quoting Jerome. The vampire had been right.

Jay collapsed dramatically to the couch. "I knew your line was weird, but I never even imagined how profoundly messed up you all are. It's no wonder Sarah had a fling with a serial killer, or that Zachary unwinds with the undead. You're all so obsessed with being perfect, you end up hating yourselves."

Zachary tried to glare at him again, but in Adia's view, the expression seemed halfhearted.

No one was perfect.

Maybe that was true—obviously it was true. Adia had

known for a long time that she was far from perfect, but she had always managed to fake it by looking to Zachary, and Dominique, and Sarah as examples of what she could be. But it had been a house of cards, and now it had all come tumbling down.

Adia jumped as her phone buzzed, announcing that she had a text message. She read it and felt her blood go cold.

No one was perfect.

But someone needed to try to be.

CHAPTER 20

SARAH FROZE. NIKOLAS had to recognize the witch in front of him. He would not have forgotten the face of the hunter who had nearly killed his brother. But Nikolas glanced at her, as if waiting for her response before he decided how to proceed.

Suddenly, the lights and music around them were surreal. Michael wouldn't attack somewhere so public, so what was he doing? He didn't even look nervous—and the Arun didn't normally bother to conceal his emotions. He looked like he should be calmly taking a stroll through the park.

"Hello, Michael," she said, trying to keep her voice even.

"Hi, Sarah," he answered. "Is this the new boyfriend?" Sarah shook her head. Michael looked at Nikolas. "I would offer to shake hands, but I don't think you would trust me that far."

"And you would trust me, would you?" Nikolas asked in the cool, controlled tone Sarah remembered well from the first time they had fought.

"I don't need to trust you," Michael answered. "I know Kendra's rules. As long as I don't attack you, if you kill me here, she'll take your head off. Do you think I would have walked up and outed myself to one of the most infamous vampires in recent history if I didn't know I had some kind of protection?"

"Nikolas?" Sarah asked.

He nodded absently and gave Michael a critical look. "You're a witch. Since when do you have any faith in our rules?"

"I'm an *Arun*," Michael answered. "Ask any Vida. We're not to be trusted, right, Sarah?"

"I always trusted you."

"Then trust me *now*," he said, earnest sincerity in his lightning-kissed eyes. "You know I think most Vida law is bull. I've got Jay Marinitch on my side, but his family is saying we have to stick to the Rights, and the Smoke witches believe refusing Vida law now will end up endangering Single-Earth. So I'm risking my ass to tell you that I'm trying to find a way out of this mess, and to ask you to help me out. You know those laws back and front. What should I do about the Rights?"

If anyone was brazen enough to flaunt their laws this way, it was Michael. He was just wild enough to gamble everything— and with a little vampiric blood in his own veins from his family, maybe he really could believe that blood alone could not turn someone into a monster.

Nikolas seemed to take his cue from Sarah's thoughts. "We are going to the theater tonight," he said to the hunter.

"Nikolas," she whispered in warning, wondering both why Nikolas was apparently inviting himself along and why he was sharing with Michael. *I would like to believe he is on our side, but he is still a witch.*

He ignored her, continuing to speak to Michael. "Perhaps we could all meet afterward, to discuss a way out of this tangle?"

If we do not give him an opportunity to double-cross us, we will never know if we can trust him, will we? he replied silently. *I think the potential of an ally among the witches is worth a bit of risk.*

"Sounds good," Michael said. "Sarah, I didn't know you liked theater. What are you seeing?"

She shrugged, not about to give him any more information than Nikolas already had.

"We haven't yet picked a show," Nikolas answered for her.

"Well, give me a call when you get out. I'll be around. Sarah . . ." Michael hesitated, his gaze lingering on her. "Well, I'll see you."

He walked out, turning his back to them as if perfectly certain they would respect the rules of this place and not hurt him. Or maybe he just trusted Sarah. She couldn't forget the expression on his face at the house. He hadn't wanted to hurt her.

Of course, that had been before the fight.

"You handled that very calmly," Sarah commented to Nikolas after Michael was out of earshot.

"He defended himself," Nikolas answered. "If Kristopher

had not recovered, I would have hunted him down, but as it is, we need allies. I will not hold against him the fact that he fought back when attacked." He paused, then added, "At least, I will not hold it against him *much*. Besides, if he knows Kendra's rules, then he knows what her wrath is like for hunters who kill without permission in her territory. I do not believe he would willingly try to fight us on the island."

"I'm not sure you fully understand how little respect Michael tends to have for authority figures," Sarah muttered. "Besides, he never mentioned anything about Kendra when we used to hunt here."

"Kendra has an arrangement with some hunters, with regards to whom and when and where they may hunt in her city. Would you have tolerated knowing of such a situation when you were still a witch?" No. Of course not. It didn't even need to be said. She wanted to believe that Michael had set up the arrangement only *after* Sarah had left the city, but looking back, she wondered if he had instead subtly steered her toward safe hunts.

In other words, he had lied to her.

Though it wasn't like he'd had any other choice when she had been a Vida.

Nikolas said, "I will ask Kendra if he has such a deal with her. In the meantime, should I even ask if you have anything suitable to wear to a theater?"

She glared at him. "Jeans and a T-shirt aren't fine, I'm guessing?"

His expression held an almost amusing mixture of horror and sorrow. "For a modern American, perhaps," he answered.

But not, she was sure, when one sat in box seats with two nineteenth-century gentlemen of Kendra's line.

"If you want to return home, I'll make arrangements," Nikolas said, judging rightly that Sarah wasn't about to say, *Oh, goody, let's go dress shopping!*

"Thanks," Sarah said. "Are you also planning to be the one to tell Kristopher you invited yourself and a vampire hunter on our date?"

Nikolas looked startled by the question. "I thought you would prefer it," he said ambiguously before he disappeared, presumably to talk to Kendra. Sarah left immediately after, not wanting to linger in a place where she had already unexpectedly run into one hunter.

She realized she was nervous, not about spending time "off" in the middle of the dangerous chaos in her wake, or about the potentially bloody confrontation with Michael that might follow, but about this essentially being the first real date she and Kristopher had gone on, and she was suddenly sharing it with his brother. The dance Kristopher had invited her to once had been a disaster even before it was cut short by the appearance of Sarah's sister, and Sarah's plea for Kristopher to leave her alone. Somehow she couldn't picture this one going any better, even if Nikolas hadn't suggested their location to people who might want to kill them.

Sarah tried to give some thought to Michael's question, but the Rights of Kin were in many ways very simple. Only the one who called them could declare them satisfied. If, goddess forbid, Dominique were killed, the decision would fall to Adia, but she would be honor-bound to fulfill her mother's wishes.

Sarah couldn't think of any power on Earth that would convince Dominique to change her mind.

She checked in on Christine, who was sleeping soundly with a much-loved-looking stuffed animal in her arms. Was she still going to want to learn to fight? Heather had comforted her about her future, to an extent, but Sarah would rather encourage Christine to be a more active agent of her own future, not as dependent as Heather.

Sarah was a half page into some notes about how she could set up an introduction to self-defense when she realized she was planning her own future. She was only writing about fighting moves and breathing techniques, but in those words was a commitment to Christine that implied Sarah would be around for a while.

She hadn't come to terms with eternity and wasn't sure she would anytime soon, but step by baby step maybe she was learning to accept that there would be a tomorrow.

She put aside the notes, which were just busywork until she could talk to Christine more, and examined the bookcase in the back of the living room, wondering if something there might help her pass the time without dwelling too much.

It had been years since she had read a book for pleasure. She didn't even know what kind of book she liked. That some of the titles weren't in English didn't help. She abandoned the bookcase and looked at the CDs instead. Here some of the non-English titles seemed familiar, like a long-ago memory she couldn't quite place.

Jake's influence.

She had just reached for one when Nikolas appeared

behind her. Sarah snatched her hand back guiltily, as if expecting Dominique to chastise her for seeking such a frivolous waste of time. She had listened to music at home, but it had always been whatever happened to be on the popular-music station on the radio; she had never bothered to consider what her *tastes* might be.

"Well, I have news you're going to like, and news I think you're going to like a lot less," Nikolas announced with a rueful expression. "Which do you want to hear first?"

"Good news, I guess," she said. He didn't look *upset*, so she imagined that the less-good news was probably one of those vampire-related things she just didn't like talking about, and not any kind of disaster.

"Kendra confirmed she *does* know Michael, and that though they do not have an explicit arrangement, he has always been careful not to break her rules. Also, she has four box tickets to *Wicked*. She thinks you will appreciate some of the themes in it."

"Uh-huh," Sarah said. She had never heard of it, so she could only hope that wasn't the bad news. On the other hand . . . "Why do we need four tickets?"

"Because she wants to meet you, and has suggested the four of us should attend together."

So much for Kristopher's idea of a light, low-pressure evening.

"I assume that's the news you figured I wouldn't like as much?" Sarah asked.

Nikolas shook his head. "I may have accidentally mentioned your *other* problem. Kendra is a woman of great class and style."

He didn't say it; he didn't *need* to say it. Like some kind of ancient, bloodthirsty mother-in-law, Kendra wanted to get to know the newest member of her line. What better way to do so than a shopping trip?

Goddess help her. She would rather face the hunters.

CHAPTER 21

ZACHARY STORMED UP the familiar weathered steps, his fingertips trembling and his breath coming quickly in what anyone who knew him would call a shockingly uncharacteristic loss of control. A streetlamp nearby flickered, and he realized he was throwing off so much wild energy he was disrupting the electrical currents.

Before putting his hand on the knob of the front door, he took a moment to pause, close his eyes and hold his breath until he stopped shaking and his heartbeat calmed. Above him, the lamp flickered once more and then died, leaving his side of the street dark.

Then, eyes cold as steel, he pulled open the door—it wasn't

locked; it was never locked—and moved into the front parlor of the small apartment.

The familiar room made his throat tighten with emotions he preferred not to analyze too closely. From the worn suede love seat and ottoman and the soft velvet curtains to the throw rug and a Tiffany lamp that cast muted light the color of roses and gold about the room and into the small kitchenette, everything was warm and welcoming. Embracing.

There were three doors from the living room entrance; now one of those doors opened and Olivia padded out, clothed in pajama pants and a camisole top of creamy silk.

Through the doorway he could see the human she had left behind on the bed. His name was Vick, and he was a hard-core blood junkie who had been living with Olivia for months. He and Zachary had met and even talked some—enough for Zachary to know he did not want to talk to him more. Vick had no family, no past he was willing to talk about and probably no future at all. His wasn't bloodbonded to anyone, but that was only because no one had claimed him so permanently. His entire existence consisted of being passed from one vampire to the next, with no desires of his own except to bleed for them.

Vick didn't even twitch when the door opened. Olivia took one look at Zachary and sighed heavily. "This again?" she asked him. She drifted closer, pausing only to close the door behind her. "After we had such a nice visit earlier."

"You took *pictures?*"

She smiled, just slightly. "Not me. But Jerome does love that camera of his."

"Adianna saw them."

"So that's the reason for today's tantrum."

She had moved close enough that now she could lay her palm against his cheek.

"Darling," she whispered, "if you intend to try to kill me, it would help if you drew a knife."

He jumped at the reminder, his hand going to the knife handle at the back of his neck. The movement was slower than usual as he fought learned reflexes.

Olivia moved her hand from his cheek and across the back of his reaching arm until her palm lay over his hand, at the back of his neck. The motion he had attempted stalled as muscles reacted to a more familiar position, relaxing and arching his throat back.

"Or," Olivia suggested, "we could do something more enjoyable."

"No."

But he couldn't make himself shove her away.

"So, what? You'll kill me?" she asked. "And then you'll go home, having destroyed the one place where you don't have to be the perfect, flawless Zachary Vida. You'll have destroyed the only person who welcomes you no matter what."

She slid against him and stretched her petite form so she could kiss his throat. Like one of Pavlov's dogs, he leaned back against the wall, his eyes closing. It was the same reflex that had shut him down at the end of the fight with Sarah.

"Did you really come here to kill me?" she purred.

"Yes."

She ran a hand up his chest. "You aren't doing a very good

job. No, hush, love," she said, laughing, when he tried to protest. "It's okay." Abruptly, she drew back, pulling a small sound of protest from his throat as she said, "Come. Sit and relax a while. We'll figure out what you can say to your dear cousin. Was she the only one who saw?"

He took a seat on the plush couch, wondering even as he did what the hell he was doing.

He had come here, once again, to kill her. He had resolved to do so dozens of times, if not hundreds, but every time she calmed him and set him off his guard.

At first, it had just been the fights. The frustration and fear and pain from the battle and any resulting injuries had faded away in the peace that a vampire's bite could bring. At that point, he had normally woken up in an empty house, long after the vampires had left.

The first time he had woken up with her still there, he had stormed out, refusing to say a word but lacking the courage to attack her.

The next time, she had woken him with a home-cooked meal and apologized that they had taken too much. *I can take care of you here, or I can take you to the healers. Your choice.* He hadn't wanted to go to the witches. He would have had to admit to them what had happened.

So he had stayed, and they had eaten breakfast together.

And it had evolved from there, over the course of what had to have been almost two years.

He enjoyed watching her as she moved about the kitchen, her feet bare and her hair down, softly humming some song he thought maybe he knew from the radio as she set a kettle on the stove to boil.

"Why haven't you killed me?" he asked.

She glanced over her shoulder as she portioned loose leaves into an old-fashioned tea ball. "I don't care for killing. I've done it when forced to," she admitted, "but this is nicer. Why? Did you want me to kill you?"

"I don't know."

She sat next to him and curled against his side.

"Poor dear. What can I do for you?"

The answer was utterly beyond him. Suddenly, he was shaking, a bone-deep trembling he struggled to control until she cooed, "It's all right. You don't have to be strong here."

It was the type of permission he didn't know how to react to. Wrapped in her arms, he could for the moment step outside the perfect Vida cage, and as soon as he did so, he was weeping.

It was all crumbling. His earliest memories were those of Jacqueline and Dominique screaming at each other, and then Jacqueline storming out. His mother wailing when they told her Jacqueline was dead, demanding to see the body for herself, leaving and never coming back. His brother, only five years old, wandering out in a quest for Mother, never to return. A parade of people leaving and getting killed, until at last Sarah was taken from them, or more likely ran from them.

Now Adia. He had seen the look of disgust on her face. If he lost her, too . . .

Olivia held him silently until the sobbing ceased; then she

stood and quietly poured the now-boiling water for the tea she had promised.

He leaned over the cup, inhaling the steam, unable to meet Olivia's gaze.

"Better?" she asked.

"Probably never."

She sighed again. "Why do you do this to yourself?"

"I owe it to my family," he replied. Had always replied. They were all he had, after all. "After Dominique took me in—"

"*Dominique*." Olivia snickered, a sound that contrasted with her normally soft, gentle image. "Even the indomitable Vida matriarch isn't perfect, you know."

"I know." He remembered all too well the terrible days after Fredrick had died. "But I have to try, the way she does."

Olivia kissed his throat, and he let her, even though he knew that if she took his blood, it would probably kill him. He had lost too much to Sarah, too recently. But of course Olivia knew that and knew she had to control herself.

Heather's words came back to him. He remembered the way her eyes had flashed as she had tried to unsettle them all by describing her life.

Would you like to know what it's like when one of them takes you? When you're in their arms and they bare your throat and drink?

I have seen hundreds of humans pass through, willing to die, willing to give up everything, just to experience that bliss. And not just humans. The Vida line isn't immune, is it?

If only she had known. If she hadn't scrambled Jay's mind so much with whatever she had shown him, Zachary's secret surely would have been revealed right then, because he knew exactly why the bloodbond had stayed with Kaleo all this time. As it was, Jay had picked up on Zachary's relationship with Olivia, even if he hadn't gotten the more sordid details.

I have seen hundreds of humans pass through, willing to die, willing to give up everything, just to experience that bliss.

When his cell phone rang, he pulled it out of his pocket and then just stared at it as Adia's number flashed on the front. He wanted to put it away. Couldn't they just leave him alone for a night?

He wasn't ready to talk to her again, to face her. He didn't think he ever *would* be ready.

Still, he hit the "talk" button and said, "Hello."

"Is now a bad time?" she asked.

Now *was* a bad time, but that wasn't really what she was asking. She wanted to know if she could talk frankly.

"Now's fine," he said. "Adia, I—"

"You are *not* going to apologize, or say a single freaking word about it right now," Adia interrupted. "If you need to talk, we'll talk when the job is done. In the meantime, I need you to pull it together and be at my back. Can you do that?"

He looked up at Olivia and met her steady gaze for several seconds before saying, "I can do that."

"Good. Then meet me at Michael's place, as soon as you can get there. We're ending this thing tonight."

Michael's apartment was in New York City. Had he located Sarah or the twins there? Adia obviously believed she knew where their targets would soon be.

"It'll take me three or four hours to get there."

"Then we'll make it by intermission."

Could it really be over so soon? And when it was done, what then? Adia knew the truth about him. So did Jay. He wouldn't be able to stay around, but he didn't know what else to be, or how else to live.

Adia hung up without saying goodbye.

"Where are you headed?" Olivia asked as Zachary put his phone back into his pocket and stood.

He shook his head. She knew he never told her outright where his hunts took him.

"Judging by the time, the people involved, and the mention of intermission, I'm guessing you're headed to Broadway," she said.

"Guess whatever you like," he said. "I have to go."

"Zimmy, you know I have no power to interfere with Kendra in Manhattan, right?"

He hesitated in the doorway and then shrugged. "I do now."

He felt calmer when he sat behind the wheel of his car. Adia had said it would be over that night. Maybe then he could rest for a while.

CHAPTER 22

SARAH FELT ABOUT as stupid as she ever had in her life, sitting in front of the full-length mirror while Christine did her hair. Christine had insisted on helping, and short of shoving her down the stairs, Sarah couldn't figure out how to convince her otherwise.

The evening had taken a surreal turn somewhere. Maybe it had been when she had tasted a symphony, or when she had spoken to Michael, but she was pretty sure it had happened somewhere on Madison Avenue, on a rack between Chanel and Vera Wang.

Going shopping for formal wear in New York with a vampire who had once founded a mystery cult in the days of the Roman republic, and who tended to chatter about the fall of empires in the tone most people used when discussing the weather, was a unique experience. Kendra referred to Nikolas as "Nikki," a nickname she claimed he hated. She also referred to Tizoc Theron, one of the most powerful mercenaries in all of vampiric existence, as her "Tizzy." The Inquisition was "a dreadful inconvenience," World War II was "a little spat" and the fall of Midnight, the vampiric empire that had reigned for centuries, was "an unfortunate event."

If Sarah lived two thousand years, maybe she would look back and agree. For now, the sentiments were almost as unsettling as the expression on Kendra's face when one of the shop managers—who had instantly appeared to wait on Kendra when she had crossed the threshold—presented a dress she found unattractive.

Now Sarah was in a turquoise dress with a neckline slightly lower than she was used to but, fortunately, no eighteenth-century-style hoops—something she had been a little worried about, given the individuals she was going with. Even better, she was almost certain no one had died in her acquisition of the dress, or in the search for shoes to match it.

"You look far away," Christine remarked.

Sarah tried to pull herself back to the moment. "Did you know Nero played the lyre, not the fiddle?" she asked. "There was no such thing as a fiddle yet." The misconception about *which* musical instrument Nero had played while Rome burned was apparently one of Kendra's pet peeves.

"Um, okay," Christine answered, pulling Sarah more truly into the correct time and place.

"I feel like an idiot," Sarah said aloud for the first time.

"You look beautiful," Christine insisted.

"Not because of that." Sarah shook her head. "Despite people trying to kill me, I just spent two hours *shopping*. With, I'm pretty sure, an outright psychopath."

"That's most of the line, or so I've heard," Christine murmured, her tone so dry Sarah actually laughed.

"Where do I fit in, then?" she asked.

Christine shrugged. "Wherever you want to. What show are you seeing?"

"I don't remember." The name had been meaningless to her. She was hoping Kendra was right that she would like it, but wasn't convinced that her tastes and those of a millennia-old vampire were likely to be the same.

When someone knocked on the door, Sarah called out, "Come in," without realizing that it was still an hour before the time Kristopher had agreed to pick her up. Christine tensed, and this time Sarah was the one to put herself between the human and the vampire, making no attempt to hide her anger.

"What do you want?" she snapped at Kaleo.

Kaleo quirked one brow. "I'm not here to hurt the girl. I just need to speak to you, Sarah."

"Out! In the hall."

The Roman looked amused by the order but obeyed, which Sarah found a little unsettling. She took a minute to reassure Christine and then followed Kaleo.

"Nikolas and Kristopher aren't here," she said flatly. "So what do you want?"

"Are you under the impression you are such a nonentity that I could not possibly be here to speak with you?" Kaleo asked.

"If you have something to say to *me*, then just get on with it. You freak the hell out of Christine just by being here."

"Kendra mentioned you are going to a show tonight," Kaleo said.

"Yeah, she does like to chat," Sarah quipped.

Kaleo glared. "Do not confuse Kendra with some of our line. She may appear outwardly indifferent to reality, but she has been one of the driving forces behind the rise and fall of empires for two thousand years. She has a fondness for Nikolas, a passing fondness for Kristopher, and thus far a limited tolerance of you that extends just far enough for her to suggest I might want to pass on a message."

The sharp words were enough to make Sarah step back and attempt to control her temper long enough to listen rationally. "You don't strike me as the errand-boy type," she said, not as an attempt to insult, but in a search for Kaleo's agenda. He did not seem likely to blithely agree to deliver messages.

"I may not like you, and I am certain you do not like me, but like it or not, we share blood. Beyond that, you risked yourself to save Heather, and I trust that you would do the same for any of our people. Your blood and your actions make you kin to me, and so I chose to come here to warn you."

Sarah nodded, taken aback by his tone and the absolute sincerity behind it. It was hard to reconcile this Kaleo with the one who had tortured Christine and killed the Ravenas' father. Of course, it was hard to reconcile the Nikolas she now knew with who she had once thought him to be.

For now, she accepted the tentative truce implied in the words.

She hadn't entirely resigned herself to the idea that living in this world meant not killing him, but if he insisted on talking like he gave a damn about his human bonds and the others Sarah cared about, she feared she might start hating him a little less.

Kaleo continued. "Michael has spoken to other hunters," he said. "They do not know what theater you will be in, but they know you plan to rendezvous with the Arun afterward. Kendra has elected not to stop the hunters forcefully, because she believes it is a confrontation that will happen sooner or later. She has asked that you try not to disrupt the play"—he quirked his mouth in a half smile—"but understands if it cannot be helped. She assures me that there would be no way to smuggle a large weapon into the theater, but would like me to remind you that not all hunters insist on engaging their prey up close, and the streets can be exposed."

Though the Vida line preferred close contact in a hunt, she knew crossbows were favored by some hunters—the kind who would shoot the silent weapon from a rooftop or a higher window, or even across a crowded theater if they could get the weapon inside.

"Do you need to sit?" Kaleo suddenly asked.

The solicitousness seemed out of place until Sarah realized she had not responded to his warning, and several seconds had gone by.

Long before their short fling, Michael had been her best friend. But this new life of hers was full of betrayals by those from the former one, so why was this surprising?

As Kendra, through Kaleo, had said, this confrontation had to happen sometime.

Inanely, Sarah said, "I had actually started to look forward to seeing the show."

"Then go," Kaleo replied. "Watch the play. I would simply advise not idling long on the streets."

He made it sound so simple. But maybe something good could come of this. She had promised Nikolas and Kristopher, and more importantly herself, that she would not give up her life, but in a public area owned by such a powerful figure, surely she would have some room to negotiate. Perhaps she could find an opportunity to plead her case. There had to be a way to convince those who had been her friends and family that she was still who she had been only days before.

"What's wrong?" were Kristopher's first words as he walked into the room where Sarah had not too long before been primping, and where she was now sitting on the bed, no longer worried about wrinkling the beautiful dress before Kristopher came to pick her up. She just looked at him. She knew he had been angry when he had left.

Since then, she had fed for the first time. She had experienced something wonderful. Then she had seen an old friend, briefly experienced the hope for forgiveness and acceptance, only to have that crushed. After Kaleo had left, she had spent nearly half an hour helping Christine calm down while trying to fight the yawning void in her own gut.

He hadn't been there for any of that, and she couldn't blame him. Nikolas had said Kristopher wasn't hard enough to force her to feed, and he was probably right. He thought that if he could only convince her this life was *worth* living, the rest would take care of itself. He didn't understand that the first steps of survival were too much to take on her own, no matter what she wanted.

He and Nikolas had left their world behind when they had become vampires. They had even changed their names to mark the transition. It wasn't as easy for her to stop being Sarah Vida, even if the Rights of Kin hadn't been in play.

"Nikolas and Kendra are going to join us for the show. I'll explain everything once your brother gets back." She didn't want to have to describe Michael's betrayal twice. Nikolas was going to meet them at home, but Kendra had said she would catch up with them at the theater, so there would be time for them to talk.

"Okay." She could still sense Kristopher's concern, but he was willing to let it drop if she wanted it to. "Where is Nikolas?"

"Talking to some contact," Sarah said, vague because he had been vague with her. "He has a plan, but hasn't explained it to me. He promised he would be back in time for the show, though."

Kristopher didn't object to Nikolas's joining them, or even ask when that had been decided, and there wasn't as much as a tendril of annoyance in response to his brother's having invited himself along on their date. Sarah realized, quite suddenly, that she was irritated by that—not that Kendra and Nikolas had invited themselves, but that Kristopher just accepted it as a matter of course, even without knowing that Kendra had been involved in the decision.

"You look good," she said, the compliment lame, but she couldn't get more eloquent words past her throat.

Of course he looked good. Kristopher Ravena in a tux was a sight to see. She was glad Nikolas and Kendra had insisted that Sarah find something "appropriate," or she would have been devastatingly underdressed. The beautiful man in front of her was like something out of a black-and-white magazine. He was standing before her, but impossible to touch.

He took the words as further invitation to change the subject and pretend everything was fine again. Holding out a hand to her, he said, "You look incredible yourself."

She ducked her head, oddly shy, and admitted, "I kid you not, Kendra took me shopping."

His eyes widened. "How on Earth did that happen?"

"Nikolas asked her to," Sarah replied. "I gather he figured I would be hopeless to prepare myself adequately on my own."

At that, there was a stab of something from him . . . not jealousy, but . . . guilt? "It's okay," she blurted out. "This whole thing has been hard on you, too. I can understand needing to get away for a bit."

She said the words before she even fully processed the thoughts she had picked up from him. Nikolas had exaggerated the amount of help Nissa had needed, but Kristopher had stalled nevertheless, needing time to go over some of the same thoughts Sarah had found slashing through her brain.

She accepted his hand.

As he drew her closer, he observed, "You've hunted."

Something made her hesitate to say Nikolas's name again,

but she knew that it was implied when she said, "I went to Phaethon."

"Oh." He reached up as if to run his fingers through his hair, and then seemed to remember that it was tied back tightly. When she had met him, Kristopher's hair had been chopped short, but it had been long when he was changed. Since he had rejoined his brother, his vampiric body had swiftly returned to its original state, and now he and Nikolas were again close enough that they were like reflections of each other. Even their auras were nearly identical, in the way they twined together.

And yet they were very different.

She had comforted him, because the feeling of his guilt had hit her so powerfully, but Kristopher was coming to the same realization she had already reached. Kristopher had changed her to save her life. Before that, at most he had intended to bloodbond her—and that only because his brother had intervened. If it hadn't been for Nikolas's struggles to get his brother to return to him, Sarah would have driven Kristopher away, and that would have been the end of their relationship instead of the beginning.

"Kristopher—" she said at the same moment that Kristopher said, "I'm sorry, Sarah."

"I should have . . ." His voice trailed off as he thought that he should have been the one to show her how to hunt, but he still hadn't reconnected with all his contacts after his fifty years away. He wouldn't have been confident enough to bring Sarah somewhere like Phaethon at a time like this. He had left to try to get his thoughts straight, at a time when he knew perfectly well that she needed him. She was new to this world, former Vida or not.

"Kristopher," Sarah said firmly. She waited until he had pulled himself from his thoughts and was really looking at her before she continued. "We both made mistakes, which caused us to end up here, but that doesn't mean you're responsible for me from here to eternity. Going to one school dance together for a date that didn't even work out doesn't mean we're destined to be together forever. I know that."

Kristopher said softly, "I was thinking earlier about what would have happened if Romeo and Juliet had woken up."

"Me too," Sarah admitted. Maybe she had picked the thought up from him. "I don't need a boyfriend, Kristopher." She started off strong, but her voice faded as she added, "But I could really use some family tonight."

This time, when Kristopher pulled her into his arms, there were no anxious doubts about responsibility and romance and failures. Kristopher knew what it meant to be family and how it felt to lose family.

I'm not losing anyone else, they both thought.

"We'll get through this," Sarah said. "I don't know how yet, but we will."

CHAPTER 23

SATURDAY, 8:01 P.M.

ADIA KNEW IT was impossible to get to New York City before the show began. Dominique had access to a private jet, but trying to scramble it, get a flight plan approved and fly into New York would take even longer than driving.

After days of anxiety riding her so tightly she thought she might explode, Adia felt strangely calm. Even with the sporadic traffic she hit, she was pretty sure she made it to New York City in record time.

Like most hunters, she tended to avoid Broadway and the general theater area of Manhattan. It was too bright, too shiny, with too many people and rarely a worthwhile hit. Being there made her nervous.

She knew what she had to do—the only thing she *could* do

if she wanted her line to survive. They were flawed; she had accepted that. But she could salvage what was left of her line, if only she could find the nerve to fulfill her vow and end this hunt.

Michael had called shortly before she reached the city, to give her the address of a Mexican restaurant not far from the theater. He had found them. Michael used a little money and a little magic to reserve the restaurant's back room for their meeting. When Adia arrived, he was eating chips and freshly made guacamole.

Zachary arrived behind Adia by less than ten minutes. He was avoiding looking at her, which was fine, since she still wasn't sure what he would see in her face. Once Jay joined them, even Michael noticed that something was up. Adia saw Jay meet the Arun's gaze and shake his head. She had never been so grateful for the telepath's interference. Now was not the time.

Adia began. "Michael, fill everyone in so we can decide what to do next."

"I was scoping spots where I thought I might hear news about Nikolas, and was lucky enough to see Sarah herself," Michael explained. "For the record, she fed, but didn't kill. Does anyone in this room really think that she would?"

Jay was the first to say no. Zachary sighed and leaned back against the counter.

Michael said, "Jay and I agree that Sarah came to the house the other day to turn herself in." He looked over at Jay, who nodded without adding anything. "We're also agreed that the most surprising part of all this is that Sarah *is* still alive. She hasn't come to us again, and she hasn't fallen on the knife. When I saw her at the club, she barely spoke. Nikolas did all the talking. I don't want her dead, you all know I don't, but I know Sarah. I want some kind of assurance that if she's living this life, it's by her own choice."

"What's your plan?" Zachary asked.

"By now, I figure they'll know we're here, but Kendra's line is arrogant enough, and takes their theater seriously enough, that they won't—"

"Wait," Zachary interrupted. "They know we're here, *why?*"

"I cleared it with Kendra," Michael replied, utterly blasé. "She has given us a green light. If Sarah or the twins present us with an opportunity, we have carte blanche to take them down. Sarah knows the way we work. If she wants to make it through the night, we won't have a clear shot. If she is being held against her will, though, we'll have a chance."

As plans went, it wasn't much, but Adia enjoyed improvisation. She was a little uncomfortable with the bit about having the approval of a two-thousand-year-old vampire, however. Granted, Michael was an Arun, but seriously—how many of her crew were in bed with the vamps, figuratively speaking?

"Could you clarify the part about your having *permission* from Kendra?" she asked. Michael had vaguely referred to that part on the phone, but she wanted to be very clear on the details before jumping into a fight.

"She doesn't want a war," Michael said. The words were an eerie echo of what Jerome had said earlier. "No one does. So we have one night to end it, however it goes, and a promise of no future retaliation from Kendra or her associates. She is somewhat unsure how Kaleo will react should the twins die, but she owns the theater we're going to hit, so she mostly gets to decide what can be done to people and vampires inside it."

"I believe Adia was looking for an explanation of the fact that you seem to be able to predict movements and contact vampires in a surprisingly friendly manner," Zachary said.

A bit hypocritical, aren't we? Adia thought cynically. Zachary was the one who had vampiric friends showing up and pulling him out of fights, after all. On the other hand, it was one thing for Zachary to have some kind of low-level patron who liked to play with him. It was quite another for Michael to be making deals with the head of the line.

"I know New York," Michael replied, not bothering to get defensive. "If you want to hunt here, you have to know the territory. Be grateful."

Jay said, "Okay, let's not start bickering. If Sarah wants to turn herself in, she'll get a message to us tonight, and we'll . . . do what needs to be done, what she asks of us. But what if she doesn't?"

"Then we'll deal with that tomorrow night," Zachary said.

Jay shook his head. "We need some kind of decision tonight. Dominique won't drop her claim just because we decide Sarah has a right to live. We need to know if we're planning to try to fight the law. We're representing three lines here. Is there some kind of plan to—"

"I've got it covered," Adia interrupted. "I'll make sure Dominique accepts however things come out tonight."

"Care to tell us this plan?" Zachary asked, but this time Adia didn't want to share. He probably wouldn't approve, and given what she had learned recently, he certainly wouldn't have the guts to do what needed to be done even if he agreed.

Jay gave her a long, even look. She didn't know what he could hear in her mind. After a moment, he said, "If you're sure."

"Whatever," Michael said. "As long as the Vida line gets rid of the hooks it's using to play with the rest of us, I'm fine with it."

"By sunrise," Adia assured him, "the Rights won't be a factor. But for now . . ." She let out a long breath as she focused herself. Where should the pieces go? "Jay, you wait with Michael on the street outside the theater. That'll put you close enough that you can try to pick up a sense of how Sarah's feeling. See if she seems scared or hopeful or angry or . . . whatever you and your line do with your mojo."

Jay nodded, so apparently the instruction was sufficient for him.

"Zachary, you wait here until we know Sarah is coming out of the theater. We don't want them to see you too early."

"What about you?"

"I'm going to scope inside the theater," Adia said. "Sarah will sense me there. Maybe she will come right to me."

"And the twins?" Michael asked. "It seems pretty certain they won't let Sarah go without a fight. Do you really want to be alone on the front line?"

"Have we confirmed whether or not we took one out in the fight?" Zachary asked. "Michael, you say you saw Nikolas. But has anyone heard anything about Kristopher?"

"Nikolas is considered pretty unstable," Michael said. "If I had successfully killed his brother, there's no way he would have looked me in the eye and played nice when I saw him."

"So it's safe to assume we'll be dealing with both of them," Jay said.

"My source implied pretty much the same thing," Adia answered. "That's why the three of you are going to be close. I want to try to see Sarah alone, but if I get into a fight, I *will* call for backup. Jay, you'll be able to sense if I'm fighting angry vampires, right? I doubt I'll have time to grab my cell phone at that point."

He nodded.

"Good. Then that's that."

She didn't have any more. Her plan was concise and specific. If anything, she was relying on Michael's assurance that Kendra had given her blessing to this, and on the ability of certain individuals to talk fast.

" 'The play's the thing,' " Zachary murmured.

"What?" Adia asked.

Zachary looked embarrassed as he explained, "It's from *Hamlet*. You know, Shakespeare?"

Adia knew of the play, but she hadn't read that one in class. "I don't read a lot of Shakespeare."

Zachary seemed like he had to gather his nerve to reply, but nevertheless he did so. "Neither did I," he said. "But I have a friend who likes it. We've seen a couple shows together."

Adia didn't know what to say to that, or why Zachary said it almost like it was a confession.

"Well, good for you," Jay replied after a long hesitation.

"Someday, Zachary, I think it would be interesting to meet your friend."

"Okay, everyone," Adia said slowly, thinking over the very few details they had. She absently patted the knife sheathed on her wrist. "Operation Seat of Our Pants is a go."

They all moved toward their places. As Adia had predicted, it was a few minutes before intermission. Broadway shows were always too long for Adia's taste. She never understood how people could tolerate just sitting, watching people walk and sing on a stage.

Was Sarah enjoying it?

Adia flipped through one of the souvenir programs, concealing her anxiety and even her presence from those around her. She had her aura masked so the vampires would not sense it, but Sarah had more than a vampire's abilities; Adia was sure she would have enough of a witch's magic left to be able to sense such familiar power near to her.

If Sarah really was still Sarah, and not just a monster, then if she knew that Adia was alone, she would come alone to talk.

Please don't disappoint me, Little Sis, Adia thought desperately. *Please.*

CHAPTER 24

SATURDAY, 8:05 P.M.

THE CROWD WITHIN the theater was made up of individuals of all ages, in all types of casual or formal wear. Sarah saw more than a few double takes from other men and women as the vampires presented their tickets and were escorted to their seats, and she was acutely aware of the image she, Kristopher, Nikolas and Kendra made as they cut through the crowd.

Sarah had never lacked confidence. She knew she was attractive, in a trendy blond kind of way. But no fine clothes or fancy hairstyle would *ever* make her match Kendra, who radiated poise and power and beauty from her golden hair—truly *gold*, like beaten metal—styled in loose curls, to the tips of her five-hundred-dollar shoes, or Nikolas and Kristopher, identical seraphim who bore no resemblance whatsoever to the poor country farmhands Nikolas had recently described them as.

Sarah knew she looked good enough on Kristopher's arm to merit envy. The four of them together, however, turned heads in awe. Kendra, Nikolas and Kristopher were obviously used to the attention, but to Sarah it was a new and somewhat unsettling response. She had spent most of her life blending in and knowing that too much attention would get her killed.

Of course, too much attention here that night might *still* be the end. Had the hunters figured out where they were? Nikolas hadn't told Michael what they were seeing, but Sarah tried not to underestimate her once kin.

She ended up sitting with Kristopher on her left, Nikolas on her right and Kendra on the opposite side of Nikolas—too close for comfort, still, but at least Kendra didn't lean over to whisper things conspiratorially in Sarah's ear like she did to Nikolas. It was almost hard to remember, with the head of their line looking radiant and excited for the show, that she had given tacit approval of Sarah's death if it did occur that night.

It was too surreal to contemplate, so Sarah tried not to. As they settled in, she wondered instead why box seats were considered *good* seats. Could anyone without a vampire's vision tell what was happening onstage from so far away? She flipped through the glossy color booklet Kendra had handed her, looking doubtfully at the strange costumes while the rest of the audience trickled in.

She waited too long to ask where and when the story took place. The lights dropped, and the music began. At first it seemed uncomfortably loud and jumbled. She struggled to make out what people were saying as they sang over each other. She made out enough of the opening song—"No One Mourns the Wicked"—to wonder what kind of "theme" the show had that Kendra thought she should appreciate. After all, Kendra had given a group of hunters permission to kill her tonight. Was this supposed to be a warning?

As the show continued, she felt like she alternated between frowning and suppressing a chuckle—but come the finale of the first act, she found herself sitting forward in her seat.

If her heart still needed to beat, she knew it would have been pounding at that moment.

She felt hands on her back and realized that Kristopher and Nikolas had both reached out to her. When she leaned back, Kristopher took her hand, and Nikolas left a comforting hand on her shoulder. The touch grounded her and reminded her where she was. She closed her eyes, not wanting to watch the characters in front of her anymore, but she could not block out the music.

Friendship, sisterhood, rebellion, betrayal. Was there a lesson she was supposed to learn here, or was she just supposed to feel like she had been kicked in the gut?

The first act ended, and Sarah stood, pulling away from Nikolas and Kristopher. She didn't even want to *look* at Kendra.

"I have to get out of here for a bit," she announced.

"Do you want—"

"I need some space," she said, interrupting Kristopher.

"If you don't want to watch the second act, we can go somewhere else," Nikolas said.

Sarah shook her head. "I want to watch the end. I just need to be alone for a minute."

"Be careful," Kristopher warned, and she nodded.

She needed to compose herself, away from the comforting and critical gaze of Kendra's lineage. She hadn't decided yet whether she *liked* the show. All she knew was that it was too much for her right then.

Before she could take herself away from the theater, seeking silence and solitude, she sensed a familiar aura. It was mostly hidden, but Sarah never could have missed it. She knew that power too well.

Adia was alone. She had found her way to an unused dressing room, doubtless using the combination of power and guile she was so good at to bypass security as easily as Sarah did by appearing in the room without walking through the halls at all. Adia had obviously been waiting for Sarah.

There were tears in Adia's eyes, though she still had enough Vida control to keep them from spilling down her face. Seeing them, Sarah felt her own throat tighten. She didn't know what Adia wanted or expected. All she knew was that seeing her sister made her heart simultaneously jump in elation and constrict with fear.

"Hey, Little Sis," Adia said with a sad smile. "I was hoping you would come say hi."

"Hi," Sarah said, uncertain how to proceed from there.

"Michael called us," Adia said. "I made sure I was the one in the theater, since I knew you wouldn't be stupid enough to walk outside. I just . . ." She drew a deep, shaking breath, and then suddenly the words were pouring out. "I wanted to see you. *Needed* to see you. Things suck without you, Sarah. I've been stuck in the safe house with a freaking Marinitch telepath. I just found out Zachary has been letting vamps snack on him in his free time. Dominique's practically disappeared. I don't think she can stand to even look at the rest of us. I want it to be over. I can get the others on my side, and force Dominique to drop her call for the Rights. I just . . ."

Her voice trailed off. Sarah stared at her, watching Adia as if her own reflection had suddenly lost control and started to weep. And Zachary! He couldn't possibly—but then again, that was what enough people had probably said about Sarah. *She couldn't possibly be involved with a vampire.*

Sarah wasn't sure which one of them made the first move, but suddenly they were both walking, and then Sarah found herself wrapped in the tightest hug her sister had given her since the day their father died. Moments of physical affection had become rarer and briefer since then, more perfunctory if they occurred at all.

This was the kind of hug she had given Sarah that day, to try to get her to stop railing and screaming and destroying everything at hand.

"I love you, Sarah," Adia said. "And I'm sorry. I'm so sorry."

Before Sarah could question why, Adia shifted just enough, and Sarah felt the knife. It slid into her back under her shoulder blade and between her ribs with the perfection only a professional hunter could achieve, not even nicking the bones to hamper its progress.

"I'm sorry," Adia said one more time. "But I gave my word. And even if the rest of the world goes to hell, a Vida's word to her kin needs to be . . ."

The words were choked off.

"Bye, Sarah."

CHAPTER 25

SATURDAY, 9:02 P.M.

ADIA LET SARAH fall. She took a step backward, and another, and halfway through the next one, she felt herself grabbed and thrown with careful violence, so that her breath was slammed out of her lungs as she struck the wall. She was able to tuck her head just enough to keep her skull from smacking the floral wallpaper, but knew she would have bruises later.

She tried to push herself to her knees to protect herself even as she struggled to pull air into compressed lungs. Her head was spinning, and for a minute she thought she was seeing double, but then she realized it was the two brothers, and if someone didn't talk fast, Adia was going to die.

The twins approached like avatars of fury.

One reached down and dragged her to her feet by her throat. "You traitorous little—"

"Nikolas!" the other protested.

"No, Kristopher," the one choking Adia protested. "You do *not* protect her after—"

"*Wait.*"

The choked voice made everyone freeze. Adia raised a hand to try to peel the fingers off her windpipe, but knew better than to draw a knife even in her own self-defense at that moment.

The twins turned to look, Kristopher leaving Adia a wide-open shot if Nikolas hadn't been careful to keep the hunter clearly under control. She wondered if Kristopher was careless, or just trusted his brother that much.

Adia had known that Sarah trusted *her* that much.

She felt her vision start to waver. The two twins became four in her blurry view.

"*Hi, Sarah,*" she wanted to say as the world went dark.

Adia saw their father's body, but before she could even think what that meant, Sarah started screaming and throwing things. Adia tried to hold on to her and calm her down, but it wasn't any use.

Sarah put her fist through one of the etched-glass panes on the doorway.

"There is no rainbow," she declared.

Another punch, another pane, another concussion of sound followed by the gentle ring of the window's remains falling to the ground.

"Sarah Vida!" their mother shouted, trying to get Sarah's attention, but Sarah wasn't listening. She seemed hypnotized by the window.

"No rainbows," she said, tears streaking her face. "It's all . . ."

Zachary was old enough and big enough that he finally managed to pull Sarah back before she could hurt herself more.

Weeping, Sarah whispered, "It's all just glass."

Adia woke with someone's lips on hers. The instinct to protest was replaced by the need to start coughing, and only when she did, and the individual above her drew back, did she realize that he had been doing CPR. She had stopped breathing.

Jerome was kneeling over her. It was remarkable that someone who didn't need to breathe could give another individual breath, but she wasn't quibbling right then. She was alive, and she was breathing, which was not the normal expected result of being throttled by an angry vampire.

That meant something had gone right.

"She's okay?" Zachary stood behind Jerome, who looked back and nodded. Adia started to ask him something, but the bruises on her throat choked off her first attempt. Zachary guessed the question and said, "I keep meaning to take a CPR lesson, but I haven't gotten around to it."

"Yeah, somewhere in your dallying about as a bleeder you got some funny survival priorities," Adia said, or at least tried to say. It came out as a squeak. That was for the best. She was happy to be alive, but the near-death experience was making her grumpy.

More composed, she managed to whisper, "Where are the others?"

"Kendra and Jay both showed up," Jerome answered. "They

tried to convince Nikolas and Kristopher that Sarah wouldn't want your neck broken. I'm not sure they were convinced, but Kendra grabbed them each by the scruff and disappeared with them. Jay took Sarah out."

"Jerome called me when he realized you had gone to talk to Sarah," Zachary said. "He said you might need my help, but I couldn't get inside in time." If Jay had gotten there first, he must have disregarded Adia's orders. He must have known what she had planned. "I think Michael is still at his post," Zachary added. "The second act hasn't even begun yet."

Funny how being strangled into unconsciousness affected one's sense of time. Logically, she knew she couldn't have stopped breathing for more than a couple of minutes, but the thoughtless darkness seemed so long.

Zachary never asked why Jerome was there. Maybe he was just used to vampires showing up to extract him from tricky situations, and assumed Jerome was once again here because of him.

Jerome, however, had known the plan; Adia had called him from the car. Now he said, "We have another rendezvous to make. Adia, are you up to it?"

"I'm a Vida," she answered. There wasn't any choice. This needed to be done now. She had fulfilled her vow.

A wave of dizziness hit her, and Jerome and Zachary simultaneously reached for her, each catching one arm.

"Would you like some ice?" Jerome offered.

"Later."

"Where are we going?" Zachary asked.

"Dominique should be at the restaurant, waiting for us," she said. "I told her to meet me."

Zachary hesitated, nearly tripping them all up. She heard him swallow before he said, "I see."

He kept walking with them, but he did so with a heavy step.

The three of them crossed the lobby. Jerome flashed a smile at the guys working there, who nodded back in a familiar way. They looked puzzled but accepted Jerome's assurances that everything was all right. Adia was unsurprised that they knew him well enough to trust his word, given she had already been told that Kendra herself owned this theater.

Zachary balked just before the doorway to the restaurant's private room, saying under his breath, "Adia . . ."

"Come on, Zimmy," Jerome said, reaching over Adia to pat Zachary on the shoulder. "Be brave."

"Did you really kill Fredrick Kallison?" Zachary blurted out.

The question sounded as if it had been simmering for a long time, possibly years.

Jerome hesitated but then shook his head.

"No," he said as he pushed the door open ahead of them. "She did."

The "she" in question, who was waiting for them, turned in the middle of a demand. "Adia, Zachary . . ." Adia could tell exactly when Dominique saw Jerome. It was as if Dominique's mind refused to process what she was seeing right away. The words kept coming, with an empty sound, despite the horror on her face. "I don't appreciate being . . . being ordered to meet you. . . . Is it . . . You said you would find Sarah tonight. . . . I . . . oh, my god."

She stumbled backward until her shoulders were pressed against the far wall, her eyes locked on Jerome.

Jerome greeted her with a smile and a "Hello, luv. It's been a while."

Zachary looked from Dominique to Jerome, his eyes going wide. He stammered, "You . . . sh-she . . . I thought . . ."

He looked at Adia with desperation, hope and resignation nakedly warring on his face. He had thought she was about to turn *him* in.

"I did as I swore I would," Adia said to Dominique. She had to clear her throat, but managed to continue at an audible level. "Now, Mother, I think we need to talk."

In the moment when Adianna and Zachary walked through the door with Jerome, Dominique Vida saw her life flash before her eyes.

She saw herself on a city street at night, a pink rose falling in front of her feet from a balcony several stories up. She saw herself blushing furiously when, after she had sneaked into a club to get away from her mother for a night, someone who should have been her prey asked her to dance. There had been a shouting argument with her mother that afternoon, and she had been angry and hurt, so she had said, to hell with it, and she had danced with him.

And over weeks, he had courted her. There had been flowers, and candy, and dancing, and one night it had seemed natural when he pulled her close to just lean her head back. She had wanted to know what it felt like. She had *needed* to know why, when she was hunting these monsters, so many humans were running after them, begging to be used as a midnight snack even if it meant risking their lives.

Now here he was, in front of her, with the daughter whose birth had made Dominique swear up and down that she could be better, stronger, *perfect,* so her children would never need to go through the same thing, and the nephew she had promised her dead sister she would always take care of.

"Frederick is a good hunter. He's a good match for you."

"He has the personality of a ferret," she replied. "I'm going out."

"You are not *going out. You have—"*

"Bye!"

Another night. She met Jerome down the street, swung a leg over his Harley-Davidson and tucked her head down against his shoulder. She wrapped her arms around his waist and made herself forget the fact that he didn't have a heartbeat. Hers beat fast enough for both of them, right?

The speed and the wind swept the sound of her mother's voice out of her ears.

He brought her to a party, to a place where she wasn't Dominique Vida, hunter, but just Dommy, a pretty girl who got to dance, and play, and flirt, and go wild. And when it was too much, and the ringing of expectations in her ears was too loud, she could go to him and bare her throat and he could make it all disappear in a haze.

"You told me you would leave me alone," she said to Jerome. Her voice sounded flat in her ears, not from Vida control, but from the absolute inability to summon any energy or emotion at all.

There was no use denying that she knew him. There was no reason Adianna and Zachary would bring him here unless they already knew the truth. She had seen the horror on Zachary's face before he had composed himself.

Now they were standing there with expressions like glass, smooth and flawless and *fake,* and she knew it because she was the one who had taught them how to wear those masks.

"I owed some favors to some friends," he answered.

"What do you want?"

Was it fear she was feeling? Or perhaps something more like relief? She couldn't tell. She felt like she was walking through a dreamscape, with someone else speaking for her.

Jerome looked at Adia, who pulled away from him and Zachary to stand on her own.

"I want you to call the lines together again, and declare the Rights of Kin satisfied," Adianna said.

"I can't just decide—"

"You called them," Zachary interrupted. "You can declare satisfaction, and it will be over."

Only upon hearing Zachary speak did emotion start to rise again: anger. She grasped at it and the righteous indignation that she had used for years to keep her moving when she wanted to stop, and let herself fall apart.

"How can you stand here, next to that *thing,* and talk to me about it being *over*?"

Adianna continued as if she had never spoken, giving her nothing against which to keep arguing.

"And then," she said, "while the lines are still there, I want you to step down as matriarch of the Vida line. If you do not . . . if you *can*not, I will call you to trial for crimes against the line."

"Dommy." Jerome stepped forward. Dominique tried to pull back again, but was already against the wall. He caught her hands, and she didn't seem to have the will to take them away again.

Once upon a time, she would have followed him anywhere. She had believed him when he had spun stories about how she could be more than just a Vida, about how she *deserved* more than the narrow life her family wanted to define for her. She had trusted him when he had said he would take care of her.

"This isn't like last time," he said.

"Please," Frederick begged her. "I can't live like this." He dropped to his knees and clasped his hands behind his back, saying that one word over and over as tears tracked through the dried blood on his face. "Please."

She yanked her hands out of Jerome's and crossed her arms tightly over her chest.

He never turned away from her, but stepped carefully back. He knew she would kill him if only she could make her body move.

After Frederick had died—after *she* had killed Frederick—she had tried to convince Jacqueline not to make the same mistake.

They had both been wild; Jacqueline had a shapeshifter boy-friend her mother never knew about, who had been trying to convince her to give up the hunting. Dominique had tried to warn her.

The last time Jacqueline had stormed out, she had been gone seven months. She had left behind her Vida blade and a note saying she wasn't coming back. Human police had found her body, with a broken neck and drained of blood, at a club she used to frequent.

"Dominique?" Adianna asked.

Dominique looked at her oldest daughter, and it was like a stranger was standing there. A few days earlier, Adianna had told her Sarah was carrying on with a creature from her school. Sarah had come home, and all Dominique had been able to see was herself, walking into the house ready for a fight, and Jacqueline, sneaking out to see her shapeshifter suitor.

"I'm going to step out now," Jerome announced. "Someone let me know how it goes."

He disappeared. Dominique stared at where he had been, unwilling to turn her gaze back to the two hunters standing before her.

"Dominique." Adianna's voice cut like a blade, even more so when she said, "*Mother.* Please. I don't know what you've done or what you think you're guilty of, but I am your daughter, and I forgive you. But you must step down. We cannot continue this way, or we will not survive."

"Would you have us give up everything we are, to survive?"

"We don't even know what we are," Zachary replied softly. He drew a deep breath and then announced, "I'm going to go ring Olivia. Adia, let me know when you're calling the lines."

He said the words with mock calm, but Dominique could see the tremble in his back as he walked away. She knew Olivia. Jerome and Olivia were a team.

She felt like she was drowning. She looked up at Adianna's bright blue gaze, and the shame and horror was bile in her throat. She realized that her nails were cutting crescents into her crossed arms. Once—or, more accurately, a hundred or more times—she would have called to Jerome when she felt like this. She would have put herself in his arms and he would have taken away every emotion she could possibly feel.

Leaving him had been hard. Not going back to him, on hands and knees if necessary, after Jacqueline's death had been nearly impossible. Every moment of every day, she had fought to keep his face out of her mind and his voice out of her head, had fought not to hear him say, *"Just relax, luv. It's all right."*

Now she had no choice but to feel it all.

She wasn't even sure she knew how.

EPILOGUE

ZACHARY BREWED COFFEE as dawn light began to seep through the windows at Olivia's apartment. Normally, he was a tea drinker, but this was a bitter morning.

Olivia wrapped her arms around his waist from behind.

"No word yet?" she asked.

He shook his head.

"Dommy will do what she needs to do," Jerome said from the couch, where he was flipping through one of Olivia's books on human psychology. "She's a practical girl that way."

"I still can't believe the two of you had a relationship," Jay remarked as he accepted a cup of coffee from Zachary. "Is this handmade?" he asked Olivia as he paused to admire the mug. She smiled and nodded. "It's beautiful." Returning to the subject, he added, "I mean, she's Dominique the indomitable. Even I can't read her most of the time. It's like the emotions just aren't there. I have a hard time picturing her as a wild, re-bellious partygoer."

Across the room, Robert laughed, a bitter, barking sound. The human had been cautiously excited when Christine had called him and asked him to join them all for breakfast and news at Olivia's. "It's like the straight-A Catholic school kid who goes out and gets drunk every weekend," he said. "You can't be that tightly wound without going a little nuts."

"More like a recovering alcoholic violently preaching so-briety," Olivia suggested. "Dommy used us to hide, and to relax. The only way to give that up was to remove any possible temptation."

"She *could* have just stayed with us, if she was that unhappy with her real life," Heather suggested sleepily from her perch on the back of the couch, behind Jerome.

Jerome shook his head. "She blamed herself for too much. Frederick followed her one night, and one of our kind grabbed him while she was with me," Jerome explained. "Olivia and I didn't even know about it until he showed up the next night with fangs, telling Dommy he couldn't live this way. He begged her to kill him. She tried to say no, but he kept telling her she *owed* it to him, that he wouldn't be this creature if not for her. It was like she shut down. I don't know what part of her she had to kill to put a knife in his heart, but she did it. Then she turned around, told me never to speak to her again and went home."

"Poor Dommy." Heather sighed. "She was such a sweet, addled little creature."

The front door opened, admitting a bruised Adia and an exhausted Michael. All voices in the apartment hushed as everyone waited to hear what she would say. She looked around, not speaking until the rest of Olivia's guests emerged from the bedrooms.

"Is it over?" Kristopher asked.

"It's over," Adia answered. "Dominique has declared the Rights of Kin satisfied. She won't hunt you anymore."

"She won't hunt much of *anyone* anymore," Michael said. "She announced that Adia's performance on this last mission was exemplary, and named Adia the new matriarch of the Vida line. Dominique has stepped aside. Evan Marinitch is convinced she is having a mental breakdown. She refuses to talk to him, so the Smoke witches are trying to convince her that a tropical vacation would be good for her health."

"How do you feel?" Kristopher asked Adia.

She rubbed her bruised throat and then shrugged. "I've been worse. How 'bout you, Sis?"

Most of them turned to look at Sarah, who was standing with Nikolas a little behind Kristopher. She stepped into the room shyly and answered, "Grateful you're as good as you are, but still like I took a knife to the heart. And I think Kendra is cross at me for bleeding on an eight-hundred-dollar dress."

Kristopher added, "It would have been nice to know the plan a little earlier."

"That *wasn't* part of the plan," Jerome insisted.

If Adia had used a Vida blade, or a weapon with any ounce of magic to it, Sarah would have been dead. Instead, Adia had fulfilled the exact vow she had made: she had tracked Sarah down and put a knife in her heart. The cold steel had sliced its way in, but a Vida witch knew how to kill, which meant she knew how *not* to. Adia had placed the knife exactly as she meant to, careful not to jar or twist it in any way that would destroy the heart sufficiently to result in death.

It was the kind of plan Adia would make. Zachary would never have been bold enough to do it. He would have been sure his hand would tremble at just the wrong moment.

"I thought you had really done it," Zachary admitted. "When I first walked in, I thought you really had killed her."

"I wish someone had explained some of this plan to *me*," Sarah said with a glare at Nikolas.

"I didn't even realize there was a plan until I saw that photo Heather left behind," Nikolas said. "I had seen Dommy when she was with Jerome, but I just remembered her as—" He broke off as he realized that several of the hunters in the room were glaring at him. "I never would have recognized her."

"There's no reason for a hunter to pay too much attention to prey," Heather remarked, "but we remember each other. I thought you had killed her, you know, when she stopped coming back." There was no accusation as she said this to Jerome. In her mind, Zachary knew, whether to grant life or death was a vampire's prerogative.

"We have to move on," Adia said, voice and body tight, as if she was fighting not to show her discomfort in her surroundings. "I just came to bring the update. I can't linger. You understand, right, Sarah?"

"I understand."

She was their leader now. Zachary doubted she would rule

with the same iron fist as her mother had, but she couldn't afford to second-guess herself. He might have a little freedom, granted by Adia's forgiveness, but she needed to keep her distance from those who had to be her prey.

For this last time, though, the two sisters approached each other, obviously both a little wary. Given how the last hug had gone, Zachary could understand why they both hesitated.

Nikolas reached out and squeezed Sarah's hand in silent encouragement. She smiled at him before she stepped forward, reaching out enough that Adia had to step back or respond.

Adia met the hug, and the two sisters embraced each other tightly.

"I'm proud of you," Adia whispered.

Sarah blinked, eyes shining with tears, before saying, "That's pretty much all I've ever wanted."

Adia half laughed, past what obviously wanted to be a sob. "I've *always* been proud of you, you idiot."

As Adia and Sarah reluctantly drew apart, Michael asked the hard question: "So, what next?" The hunters gathered to leave together. Zachary hadn't needed to be at the meeting—it had been for the leaders of the lines—but he did need to eventually show his face to other witches again. "I mean, we have a truce right now, but next time I walk into a party before the Devil's Hour, I'm not going to walk out and let people die because some of my vampiric in-laws are there. Do we come up with some kind of rules of engagement?"

"Olivia and I plan to join SingleEarth," Sarah said. "That way there will be no reason for anyone to feel conflicted about visiting this apartment, or knowing its location, or maintaining contact with either of us. My magic is all messed up from the vampire blood, but Caryn has offered to help me learn how to use it again, in a way that's more focused on healing than fighting. SingleEarth always needs healers."

Olivia had already discussed that part of the plan with Zachary. *I already mostly obey their rules*, she had said. *It's no sacrifice for me to make it official.*

"The rest of us have managed this long without ending up on a hunter's blade," Nikolas said. "You do what you feel you need to do. You can ask Zachary how the game works when your prey is your kin and is watching your back."

"It's complicated," Zachary admitted.

But Jay shook his head. "No . . . I don't think it really is. You're used to living by all of the Vida rules. Some of us are used to more natural laws, where the hunt is about the hunt, not anger or vengeance."

"That's a very predatory outlook, for someone named after a songbird," Michael observed.

"Maybe." Jay grinned. "I've always been close to birds. I understand them. They speak to me. But my bonded companion is a lynx. We all have to find a balance somewhere."

Zachary stared at the Marinitch witch with surprise, trying to picture him prowling through the woods with one of the big cats by his side. It was hard to imagine in a way that didn't involve his animal companion hunting him.

"Balance," he said out loud. "That would be nice."

"Much better than perfection," Sarah agreed.

ABOUT THE AUTHOR

AMELIA ATWATER-RHODES wrote her first novel, *In the Forests of the Night*, when she was thirteen. Other books in the Den of Shadows series are *Demon in My View*, *Shattered Mirror*, *Midnight Predator*, *Persistence of Memory*, *Token of Darkness*, and *All Just Glass*. She has also published the five-volume series The Kiesha'ra: *Hawksong*, a *School Library Journal* Best Book of the Year and a *Voice of Youth Advocates* Best Science Fiction, Fantasy, and Horror Selection; *Snakecharm*; *Falcondance*; *Wolfcry*, an IRA–CBC Young Adults' Choice; and *Wyvernhail*. Visit her online at ameliaatwaterrhodes.com.